The Incredible T̶a̶ Time Travelling Danny Radcliffe
(Son of Bob)

Any resemblance to real persons or other real-life entities is purely coincidental. All characters and other entities appearing in this work are fictitious. Any resemblance to real persons, dead, alive or yet to be, or other real-life entities, past or present or future, is purely coincidental.

Prelude: Who, Where, Why and What.

The year is **12,020**AD. The Earth is tired and, while not quite dying, is damaged – there are few natural resources left. Mankind is much reduced with a population significantly under one billion, but still technologically highly advanced.

There are 3 types of humans. By far the majority are **Mods** (Genetically Modified); still with significant proportions of human DNA, they are able to reproduce and were originally engineered for specialist tasks back in the 'Great Leap Forward', between the fourth and seventh millennium.

Mutants; carrying naturally occurring mutations, often created as Mods interbred, which provided advantage and therefore became dominant features through natural selection.

And finally, **Naturals**; extremely rare remnants of natural humans, but even these carry the genes of the original gene selection and enhancement programmes.

There is no animosity nor hierarchy between the groups – racism and other forms of bigotry were eradicated thousands of years earlier. By the middle of the third millennium, most natural humans were generally brown (sex, time and the ability to travel acting together to create almost completely uniform human characteristics), and once gene editing and preferential selection became the norm, intelligence came as standard, and so stupidity, racism, religious fanaticism and ignorance were consigned to the history books.

Natural humans, despite being generally less able than the other two groups, tended to be treated as mainly funny and cute...If one is spotted in public they are usually asked for holo-selfies or avatar-swap. Mutants and Mods post holo-pictures or videos on their profiles of Naturals doing particularly stupid things such as struggling to operate MOD specialist heavy machinery or kick a football! Generally considered hilarious, there are literally billions of these kinds of videos all over the Quanta-web.

So, this is generally a peaceful Earth. Occasionally small wars and skirmishes break out amongst mutant groups, but they have little chance of standing up to the government platoons and quickly subside.

The thing that ultimately threatens this world more than anything else, is boredom, isolation and stagnation...Once the laws of physics were understood (by pretty much everybody) and the great technological challenges were overcome, it became obvious that there was to be no great 'galactic empire' and mankind was largely trapped on Earth until Earth was no more, which slowly eroded away any motivation for doing anything much. This was reinforced by the total lack of any communication with any other alien life-forms despite significant attempts to find them over several millennia.

So despite being the most advanced living things known to exist anywhere in the Universe and any time in Earth's history, people tended towards lives of idle hedonism, whiling away time doing the things people have always done, such as exercising, drinking, socialising, drinking, sex, drinking and listening to music. This was especially the case at Dizzy Gill's Jazz Haus, the last jazz club on Earth in the district of Man-Hat-On.

The club was owned by Kapitan Swan Shadow and his partner in business and life, Red 'Dizzy' Gill, a beautiful and tall Mod who's looks camouflaged her incredible strength and resilience.

They first met when Shadow, a former genetically modified government soldier from the elite 'Invisibles Ops' Shadow Core, was clearing out a rebellious renegade mutant gang in the Man-Hat-On district. Shadow Core troops were originally genetically modified to produce Vantablack (blackest black) pigment in the skin, were cold blooded and therefore almost completely undetectable in the dark.

Swan found Red hiding from the mutants in a depleted underground petrol tank in the junk yard surrounding the club, living off the fumes. Red was principally based on hydro-carbon rich biology; and her type of Mod had been designed to be able to work mining fuel rich deposits on large asteroids. She came back to Earth after the work dried up when it finally

became uneconomical as more of the mods who depended on it switched to lower calorie alternatives. Living off the fumes in a fuel tank was a bit like a natural human living off neat Vodka; possible but not necessarily recommended.

Shadow immediately fell for Red and stayed with her to help 'recuperate', and together they took over the ancient bunker like building that had been the renegades HQ. Over a number of years the couple turned the place into a bar and music venue (obvious to both that this had been its original purpose), which became Dizzy Gill's Jazz Haus...maybe not the best move for a recovering fumaholic, but it worked for them.

As well as being a soldier, Shadow played an antique instrument, known as a 'saxophone', which was also coated in Vantablack and made out of an incredibly tough alloy forged during the Great Leap Forward (**GLP**). It had been in his family for generations, and was presented to his ancestor Admiral Sigur Shadow, along with a copy of 'The Great American Songbook' – an antique produced from the same material as the sax, but with incredibly thin pages and containing almost 500 songs from the golden era of jazz.

Admiral Shadow was leading the force which escorted the HSS2 starship (the only manned Starship ever built by mankind) out to Jupiter when it was launched in the middle of the fourth millennium; now a name etched in the history books along with the captain of the Starship, Capt Daniel Radisson. The Admiral famously said that he never understood why he was given the sax as he didn't play, but as it was passed down the generations it became expected that one of the children would continue the tradition of learning the instrument, the songs in the songbook and spreading the word about the amazing historic music known as 'jazz'…

For Shadow the instrument was a fundamental part of who his persona and he played it every day, even throughout his years as a soldier.

Under Shadow's tutorship, and by watching hundreds of hours of holographs on the Quantaweb, Red learnt to play the syntar (a combination of guitar and synth) ; and so, once 'Kato' was recruited on drums, 'Chill' on the bass, and 'Georgia' (a natural human!) on keyboards, the My Funny Quarantine band was formed. The name was a joke, playing on the name of one of the tunes in the Songbook, as well as the constant lockdowns that still plagued the Earth even in the thirteenth millennia...

MAN-HAT-ON

Chapter I: Kapitan Shadow

Kapitan Swan Shadow climbed out of the taxi into the hammering rain and dashed through the outer gates of the scrapyard and towards the angular bunker like building that had been his home for some ten years now. Tall overgrown wisteria drooped down over the top of the junk, emerging from small clearings, heavy with water laden purple flowers, bowing down and fighting the blustery wind. He was carrying two cases, both a dark grey titanium alloy; one a standard rectangular briefcase and the other, for anyone who knew such things, the unmistakable outline of a saxophone. He was dressed in a long grey coat that the rain slid off without leaving any trace of moisture and he appeared to glide effortlessly across the yard, dodging the puddles gathering in the gravel potholes between the piles of twisted metal.

However, his most striking feature was the impenetrable black of his face and hands, which looked like holes floating in mid-air. Apart from his eyes which glistened just ever so slightly, it was almost impossible to focus on any features at all. As everyone knew as soon as he appeared, Kapitan Shadow was a former genetically modified soldier from the elite special forces 'Shadow Core'; his skin naturally produced Vantablack pigment, the blackest black. He was a perfectly balanced pinnacle of 'mod' development and innovation, and the squad had been at the forefront of government security requirements for over seven millennia, with pure lines going right the way back to the early days of the 'Great Leap Forward'.

In his head he was stomping, but to any of those milling about the yard, he appeared to be gliding without actually moving any limbs, genetically purpose built for silent combat. He arrived at the front door of his club 'Dizzie Gill's Jazz Haus', which was also the home he shared with Red 'Dizzie' Gill, his life and business partner, who was stood outside the door sheltering from the rain and drawing on a LPG (Liquid Petroleum Gas) vape.

Red was also genetically modified, designed to live in hydro-carbon rich environments (mainly asteroids). She was incredibly tough, and could quite happily consume as much propane as any mod twice her size.

She tutted, flames licking around her lips…

'Arch has called in – he can't make it again – local lockdown in Cheadle Doom'.

Shadow rolled his eyes, which just had the effect of making them faintly twinkle ever so slightly more…

'Fracking Frack, that guy is useless – he knew the lockdown was coming, why didn't he get out sooner…honestly why do we use that guy?'

'Because he's the best' shrugs Red 'and the only one who really knows his way around our antique sound system'

Archold was the house sound engineer – an antique tech nut, cross dressing mutant who was virtually invisible, which can be tricky when trying to catch his eye from the stage. He became part of the team in the very early days of the club, helping Red and Shadow put the system back together and get the club open. The problem with Archold was that he could very easily be distracted by the next bit of ancient tech to be discovered and his skills as a renovator were in constant and high demand. In fact, his duties as sound engineer were very much a hobby, something that Red had recognised long before.

'It's alright, I have put a post up on Modbook, there will be someone else out there who can do it – we can't just rely on Arch forever anyway'.

'Oh yea, this stuff – this tech isn't found anywhere else on Earth – have you ever seen anything else like it...I will bet you a gallon of butane no one will turn up who can even turn the thing on...'.

Red shrugged, there's always a way and always someone who has the skills required.

Red and Shadow had been living in the club for just over ten years now. They met when Shadow's team had been deployed to clear some renegade mutants from the site and he discovered Red hiding in a disused fuel tank. As soon as Shadow saw the building he knew his future lay there, he didn't know why, just an over-whelming compulsion to stay and fulfil his life-long dream of opening and owning a 'jazz club'.

He quit the platoon and moved to Man-Hat-On to start the club. He had always wanted to open a jazz club, it was the other part of his 'calling' that had always been in him, ever since he had been a child and given the Vanatablack Sax, the remarkable family heirloom that had been passed down through many generations of the Shadow family.

The pair walked into the club – the lights were on and the rest of the guys in the house band were already there.

The place had the same warm musty smell it had the very first time he entered it over ten years ago. Back then, it was a very different circumstance; a whole band of mutants were hid in the place, and although he didn't know it at the time, they had headed down into what had been the old beer cellar where they were hoping to avoid Swan's platoon. Even then, with the red morning sunlight catching the dust as it streamed through a tall arched window, glazed with ancient frosted glass with faint etchings still visible, the place was packed with history and character.

The wooden floors were dark and dry with age, endless footsteps wearing away the surface of the ancient timber. And, at the far end, the unmistakable raised platform of a remarkably deep stage under a simple but elegant proscenium arch. Remnants of curtains hung on the steel trusses at the back of the stage and ancient clamps still held onto broken lamps. A single ball covered in tiny mirrors twisted ever so slightly backwards and forwards as the air moved around it, suspended from a lighting truss which crossed the entire width of the room in front of the stage. The mirrors sent tiny motes of light skittering across the ceiling and wall, making dust sparkle and outlining the rest of the arched windows, all boarded up, along the full length of the room.

It stopped him in his tracks, his weapon hanging in his outstretched arm, it was an ancient music venue. He knew it to his bones, hundreds or even thousands of years ago (this was one of the oldest industrial districts on Earth) this had been, not just a music venue, but a real genuine one hundred percent authentic jazz club. At that moment, he knew that this was the place he had dreamed of, had spent his whole life looking for, and no bunch of mutants was going to stop him now.

The memory flickered back, it felt so different now as he stood there with his saxophone case hanging at the end of the same arm that had once held his rifle. They had really fitted it out well, he thought to himself.

Once he had met Red, and got Archold involved in the project, the desire to return the club to its former glory had been all consuming. After doing extensive research, they began to renovate the main space. Initially painting the walls a deep and dark Victorian blue green, they began sourcing rich red and black velvet fabrics for the curtains (Red said it represented them both and that should be the colour scheme), and genuine wooden small round tables and chairs to fill the old dance floor in front of the stage.

The bar was crafted out of wooden boards which they found in the cellars and, while they had a rustic feel, once polished up they looked truly beautiful, with deep ancient dark grain running like the current of a fossilised river for the full length of the surface, enhancing the sense of history of the place.

Archold had wandered into the venue one day, and just started helping out. As a whizz with ancient electronics he was invaluable, re-wiring everywhere and fitting the remarkable sound system that he had sourced from a specialist electronica antique trader in Mexico City many years before. As he said, he had just been waiting for the right time and place to install somewhere, but it had to be somewhere special, not just any bar.

Shadow stopped reminiscing just in time to see Chill, the bands bass player, carrying gear from out of the store, and Kato spinning around on his drum stool in the middle of the stage, looking through the bits of hardware and electronics scattered around him and deciding what to add to the drum cage for tonight's show. Both were mutants, combinations of many different types of mods that had interbred over the millennia before the genes themselves twisted them into their own unique pattern and characteristics. Chill was dark, not as dark as the Kapitan, but undoubtedly had some Shadow Platoon blood in him, but was also much heavier and had long dreaded brown hair. Kato was unbelievably thin, and his legs were as dextrous as his arms which he used to great effect behind the drums.

Georgia, the keyboard player, had yet to arrive, but that was also pretty normal. She was the USP of the band – slight, delicate and beautiful; she was a natural human – incredibly rare and a huge draw for the club in her own right. Also, she was brilliant. Despite her small stature, as soon as she got behind the keys the band pulsated. It was difficult to know why, she just provided an energy that was unique, phrasing that sat off the beat in a way that shouldn't work, but just did.

Archold had collected her a selection of rare and very old keyboards, including a GLP era rebuild of a classic Hammond Organ, which Chill organised around the old Steinaha grand piano which stayed in the corner of the stage.

Natural humans existed in a funny social space within society in the thirteenth millennium.

Generally seen as fairly useless, but also hilarious, and kind of cute, the Quantaweb is packed full of holo-videos of them doing ridiculous things. It had now been banned to get them to do anything that was really dangerous for the sake of an amusing video, but there was enough content out there to keep the enthusiasts going for a lifetime, as well as simulated computer generated film that was often presented as if real, until Modbook took it down or flagged it up as fake.

Mods were originally (back in the fourth millennium) developed to be able to work in many tough environments and they were unable to reproduce, but after the 27th Great Pandemic, when the natural human young population was rendered almost completely infertile by the most horrific virus of all, it was decided that the best means of guaranteeing the future of mankind in any form was to relax the restrictions and allow reproduction genes into the Mod genetic pool. It led to the greatest period of development for humanity in history, when huge leaps in knowledge and ambition drove mankind through a remarkable period of technical and intellectual growth, in all its expanding forms, along for almost three thousand years.

One of the strangest outcomes of the relaxation, and a footnote in the history books, was the final demise of football. It turned out that within some element of genetic base code carried within all Mods (derived from a broad range of human gene banks collected from a wide selection of some of the most remarkable humans who ever lived), was an innate ability to be able to play football incredibly well. Almost every Mod could outplay even the best human footballer, which just sort of took the fun out of it for natural humans. Even more annoyingly, Mods were just not all that interested in it, apart from watching

Naturals being so rubbish at it, but the howls of laughter from the stands didn't go down well on the pitch either. Being good at it just wasn't a thing, and so it became a minority sport and eventually disappeared.

On the other hand, most people agreed that the musical feel of a natural human was rarely, if ever, surpassed by a Mod or Mutant. And so the people flocked to see Georgia play and it kept the place busy, while making her in-expendable, and Georgia knew it.

Suddenly, there was a knock at the stage door. Expecting it to be Georgia, Shadow walked over and threw it open with a big smile, his teeth looking like mercury and faintly shimmering in the dark. It immediately fell as he was surprised to see someone completely different. In the doorway, casually looking around the yard, stood a small, bespectacled and definitely natural human man with an enigmatic smile and small black French beret. He looked up at Shadow.

'Hello, I'm Danny – I've come about the ad...for soundman...on Modbook' he explained, before casually walking past Shadow and into the club.

Chapter 2 - A New Arrival

Despite being an elite soldier and a pinnacle of genetic engineering and a tough as nails asteroid mining Mod, Shadow and Red found the setting up and running of a jazz club remarkably complicated and challenging. There was just so many things to think about, not least all the different ways the money could go out the door. There was the obvious cost of keeping the place stocked up and paying the musicians, but on top of that all the various licenses, copyright charges, repairs and maintenance and technical costs meant that the profit to turnover was just so remarkably small. In the early days both he and Red would have to go over the figures several times just to convince themselves they had got it right. In the end, once Georgia had been recruited, they just put the prices up and hoped for the best, and sure enough the best came right along, customers piled in and all was good.

However, the value of what Archold also brought to the project in the early days could not be under-estimated. Red, who was generally more numerate, was very well aware that in many ways he had made the difference between success and failure. His knowledge and enthusiasm meant that things were fixed for a fraction of the price it would cost in a commercial repair shop, and so she took very good care of him. Suffice it to say she had realised some time ago that the club could not rely on him night after night and that they really did need to get someone else who could also do the job.

Arch's only real problem was he was such a crazy eccentric it drove Shadow mad; and therefore Red was constantly having to navigate the relationship between them both, as both were essential to keeping the whole thing going. Red also knew that it could not be sustained and eventually it would break, and so had been reaching out for some time to try and find a replacement sound engineer, which would protect the club from the risk of Arch walking out…

—————————————————————

Shadow turned around on his heel as Danny headed over to the sound desk, leaping nimbly up onto the raised platform and peering through his peculiar round spectacles at the various dials and digital displays before ducking down and out of sight into the web of wires and cables underneath.

'Woaa - Are you sure you know what you are doing – this is pretty rare kit!'– Shadow suddenly felt that maybe he should have treated Archold with a bit more respect after all…

Danny's head appeared over the top of the box 'yes, yes, don't worry – I am very familiar with this kind of system, just need to check a few things' he said whilst glancing around at the various graphic displays and peering over the top of his glasses towards the speakers hung above the stage.

He jumped out from behind the desk, striding purposefully (in fact a bit over excitedly Shadow thought) to the amp room where the power distributors were placed and happily started flicking the switches on. The system thrummed into life in the recognisable order that Arch was always careful to emphasise 'This system can't be just 'turned on' – it's a power up procedure – just like one of your space planes' which always had Shadow rolling his eyes…

By the time the powering up sequence was complete, Danny was back at the desk and dialling up a tune that Shadow instantly recognised from his copy of the Great American Song Book, but featuring the most silky voice he had ever heard.

'Nat King Cole' said Danny, seeing Shadows face out of the corner of his eye, before continuing to concentrate on the screens in front of him and occasionally disappearing back underneath the desk.

'Where did you get this?' said Shadow 'I don't know this recording...of this tune' – this sounds...really old..!'

'Oh, I have a lot of very old recordings...it's my...interest.' Danny smiled a rather enigmatic smile and turned up the music 'fantastic isn't it'

'Yes' said Shadow 'Yes it is'.

'It's from the early days of the Anthropocene, you know, the Industrial Revolution...before computers and interplanetary travel...' Danny raised his eyebrows, enquiring if Shadow knew anything of what he was talking about.

'Yes, I know when – the end of the second millennium, the golden age of jazz...I know all about it' said Shadow, slightly impatiently...he ran a jazz club after all.

Chapter 3: All the way back

Shadow was inevitably caught up with the history of music, culture and especially jazz, and how it was that it had even become a thing all those millennia ago. He often wondered what it must have been like in those last days of the second millennium when big gas guzzling cars and factories poured out their poisons directly into the air!

He imagined the early clubs in the giant megacities and the huge crowds of natural humans of all different races and colours with no mods or mutants amongst them, working all day most days and cramming into the bars, clubs and restaurants to listen to that hot new sound at night. It was all so long ago and so much had changed, but also so little as people still came out to hear the sound of jazz music; so different to the sterile computer-generated junk played on most of the trash Quantum-web stations still operating.

The Anthropocene pretty much covered the last ten thousand years – in fact all the years since the very beginning of the Industrial Revolution, and the geological impact of that on the planet.

While the end of the second millennium introduced industrialisation, it was in the early stages of the third millennium that this transferred into a global move to an information based economy. This began the democratisation of access to information and initially undermined the role of 'the expert' as knowledge became so freely and widely available.

However, without the intellectual skills to apply the knowledge, this became a blunt tool at best and dangerous at worst. The third millennium can be defined as an era of catastrophic lurches between inter-governmental agendas, resulting in significant damage to the environment, global warming followed by ill-conceived geo engineering interventions resulting in a mini ice age and a constant series of plagues and pandemics, socio-economic collapses and terrible wars around unproven religious or social ideology.

It was not until the end of the third millennium that Professor Joseph Onabule used his new found fame to proclaim that it was finally time to abandon democracy and the political systems which had dominated nations for centuries. He endorsed and then engineered a move to a system far more conducive to piloting 'Starship Earth' than the one which had been employed from before a time when anyone realised the Earth was moving at all; a self contained bio-sphere floating in an almost eternal abyss.

He successfully pointed out what everyone pretty much instinctively knew already; which was to say that those who put their hands up first and spoke the loudest were almost certainly the ones least fit to run things, most specifically nations or an entire planet. He pointed at a long history of dim-witted (his term which he used extensively and very often to the subjects faces, which given he was regarded as the most intelligent human who ever lived, was particularly effective) politicians who had almost no idea of the theories or mechanisms that had driven mankind through the troubled waters of the third millennium, and indeed that their misunderstanding was almost entirely responsible for the worst of it.

It can't be right that because a single person is elected by an under-educated majority (he really could say things like this and get away with it), that this was some excuse for being allowed to say (or think) things that were clearly factually incorrect. He propositioned that it had to be that anyone who fundamentally did not have the skills to deliver on their brief, should be dismissed as they would be within any other large scale industrial structure. Pointing to the honed 'command and control' model employed by NASA (with whom he had worked for many years) he made a clear and rational argument for zero tolerance for intellectual incompetence and that a new model needed to be put in place, based on a non-executive elected board (elected by the electorate) whose only job and authority was to appoint a responsible and professional executive parliament, and dismiss individuals if they proved to be not up to the task, or made inexcusable mistakes.

Onobule proposed that these positions should be recruited through the most rigorous process; and should be the best paid jobs on the planet, attracting the very best people who were competent not only in their own disciplines but also how that integrated with others, and above all be the most intelligent people alive at any one time. In fact, rather like jury duty, it was essential that those possessing the characteristics should contribute ten years of their life to the service of mankind, in return for which they would be very well paid and provided with considerable resources to develop their area of research once they had served their term.

After the catastrophic attempt at geo-engineering and the mini ice age at the end of the millennium, caused by the monumentally incompetent President Vlad MacLeod, the already shrunken human population was ready for any alternative and finally voted in a world parliament on a platform of change based on Onabule's ideas, which after two years of recruitment dissolved itself to begin the new governance structure.

So began the long slow climb out of The Great Decline and for another thousand years mankind stabilised around a model of long term strategic development and planning rather than short term misconceptions and false doctrines, and this proved to be a hugely successful model which formed the secure governance and leadership which would ultimately lead to the era known as The Great Leap Forward.

Danny put on another track, this time an instrumental featuring the blistering saxophone of John Coltrane..

'Do you know this one' asked Danny

'Yep' replied Shadow, genuinely amazed 'Giant Steps'. Shadow couldn't help thinking that it was quite possible that they were the only two humans on the entire planet who would recognise the tune, and how remarkable it was that there they both were, in the same room at the same time.

At that moment Georgia walked into the room 'This sounds crazy man – who is it?' she said before seeing Danny 'and who's this?' she said nodding at the clubs new engineer and fellow natural human...'

Chapter 4: Foggy Daze

While, in the thirteenth millennium, Natural Humans were considered to be pretty weak (and very rare) by the majority Mod and Mutant populations, Georgia did not quite fit that mould. Sure, she was pretty tiny, certainly much smaller than the average, but her aurora told a very different story. Every inch of her small frame said 'solid steel'. Sporting traditional eastern tattoos on her arms and legs, she had a slightly oriental look, which in itself was remarkable as it was extremely rare for any Naturals to carry a racial trait. Most likely a co-incidental genetic throwback, but one that Georgia exploited to increase her mystique and local celebrity status.

Shadow was not immune from her ability to put on the pressure with little more than a look, and often danced around her quite tentatively. Red often took the piss, to which Shadow defended himself by saying it was just out of respect for her remarkable musicianship, but they both knew that whatever made her a great player, also made her a very intense individual to be around.

'So who are you?' Said Georgia while chewing around a piece of gum.

'I'm Danny, your new deputy house engineer' he said with a smile before putting out his hand 'nice to meet you Georgia – hell of a keys player'.

Danny's face was a full smile and did not carry any trace of being even remotely intimidated by Georgia's initial cold stare, which surprisingly relaxed into a soft smile. 'Do I know you?' she asked…

'I've heard you play' said Danny continuing to smile while avoiding the question…'and very much looking forward to hearing you again!' He nodded at the stage 'I think the guys have most of your gear set up, just give me a nod if you need anything else'. Danny gave a big grin and span around and was off again, running cables and mics to mic stands and generally doing what tech's do and musicians rarely understand. Georgia continued to smile – she took an instant liking to the guy, which was quite unusual given that she was often cautious around other naturals when she bumped into them. She headed for the stage, switching on the various keyboards before turning to the piano and playing a blistering run down the keys, just so there is no doubt that everyone knew she was ready to start playing.

Shadow looked on, smiling to himself as the two diminutive figures moved apart, both sporting a beret cocked to one side and clearly both with bucket loads of self-confidence. It's going to be fun watching how this plays out, he thought to himself.

The night got off to a great start. It was busy from the get go, people piling through the doors in a steady stream and cramming the bar while others headed to the tables in front of the stage. Red was dashing around, making sure that everything was just right and adjusting the house lights while talking to Valentine, the Venue Manager.

Danny was also zipping about, making last minute adjustments to mic positions and cables and generally tidying up the stage. Everyone had taken an instant liking to him and he was showing no signs at all of 'first night on the job' nerves.

As the clock ticked around to 9pm the band moved towards the stage while the stage lights were still dark and started tuning their instruments, re-ordering the music and making their own last-minute checks and adjustments.

As the lights came up, a magical glow of amber and red, Chill stood like a hulking mass at the back of the stage with his double stack of amplifiers, which he ran incredibly quietly for there size, but which always sounded full, fat and round. He swapped between an electric double bass and synbass throughout the gig – both proportionate to his impressive size.

Kato sat within his drum cage – three titanium circles locked together with an array of percussion and electronic gadgets hanging around the top half with a slightly more traditional electronic kit around the bottom. His seat was articulated, allowing him to spin around within the cage; almost to the point he could lie on his back. His incredibly long and dextrous limbs could reach all around the kit and he used this to incredible effect, often sounding like two drummers playing at the same time.

Red always stood stage right and set back a little and in her own pool of red light. Tall, powerful and beautiful. She knew her place, and her place was keeping a lock on Kato and Chill, making sure they stay tight and focussed and don't head off on their own tangent. Even though she was the least experienced and proficient member of the band, she provided the glue and the discipline and in many ways was the actual band leader.

Then Georgia sat stage left, in front of Chill and level with Shadow at the edge of the stage. Surrounded by vintage keyboards she smouldered with an intensity that drew all eyes to her. She had star quality, whatever that is; people just loved to watch her play. She moved between sitting down and standing up, beret cocked to one side and dark purple lips, arms exposed and covered in tattoos. As much as Shadow was black, she was glowing in white.

In the middle of it all stood Shadow, almost completely invisible in the half light of the stage, his Vantablack sax hanging around his neck. He quickly checked his reed and his tuning. He wore a grey suit which shimmered ever so slightly in the light. Despite the musicianship, the band knew how to look good and they played to their strengths. Shadow often felt like he was driving an armoured vehicle, pushing on and on with the all-powerful beat, pulsating through the club and stopping for no one.

The stage lights brighten and without hesitation Kato brings in the beat of 'Foggy Daze', one of the audiences favourites, and within two bars the band are in full flow, a gentle powerhouse that instantly fires up the audience who break into applause…

Chapter 5 : Shadow takes flight

The house lights came up as Shadow opened his eyes and looked up at the crowd – the whole room was electric, everyone was on their feet and shouting and cheering. The band stand to take the applause and they all knew it had been a truly special show, one of those times when everything locks and becomes one thing; an unstoppable musical machine, throbbing and flying at the same time, all the whole making so much more than the sum of the parts, the kind of moment musicians live for.

Shadow looked to the sound desk, eyes blurred with sweat, and saw Daniel standing, peering over the digital lights and grinning from ear to ear. One hell of a first gig Shadow thought…what a way to start a new job. He gave Danny a nod and a quick smile before turning around and headed off the side of the stage and back towards the dressing room, sweeping up his sax from it's stand as he glided passed, tossing it from one hand to the other with an effortless flick of the wrist.

'Amazing gig tonight guys' he said as he entered the dressing room 'Georgia – it was an honour to be on the stage with you'. He gave a small bow in Georgia's direction.

'Thankyou, but to be honest, it was the sound – I could hear everybody as if they were in my head, it was amazing, especially the monitors, but I think it was just as good in the room' Kato, Red and Chill all grunted in agreement, Chill's head wrapped up in a big white towel, 'Yep, you've got to give that Danny kid his due' he said 'The sound was something else…'

'Where did you say the guy came from?' asked Kato

'He answered an advert I put on Modbook' answered Red, ' he came back almost as soon as I put it up..must have been keen'

'Maybe Archold lined him up – would be typical of him to be honest' answered Kato.

Georgia edged over to Shadow while everyone was considering what Archold might be up to at the moment.

'Did you see the glow on your sax?' she asked 'like gold threads on the rods – I've never seen that before, don't think the others could see 'cos they were behind you, but do you think the Vantablack is wearing off or something? It might have been the lights but kind of looked a bit weird'

Shadow looked down at her, not really sure what she was talking about but now he thought about it he had got a sense of a faint light just below his line of sight.

'No…maybe, I wasn't really thinking about it but I don't think it's wearing thin..I suppose it could be, it is over 8000 years old after all'.

Chapter 6: HSS2 (3792AD)

Admiral Sigur Shadow walked towards the bridge of the HSS2 to meet the Captain. The most advanced space ship ever developed, and the first manned vessel from Earth to be able to truly hold the title 'Starship', the HSS2 corridors gleamed white with holographic screens situated along the corridors in-between the expansive windows which framed the deep black of space.

The amazing view of the Jovian system hung in the distance, the Moon Io directly in the ships line of site, it's mottled surface glimmering in the reduced sunlight with a sulphurous yellow and golden brown, like melted bubbling brown sugar on a creme brûlée. Jupiter itself sat floating in the distance, a vast disk of spinning orange, brown and white gas with storms and cloud banks which would easily swallow the whole of the Earth.

The Admiral's approach to the HSS2 in his own interplanetary military cruiser, had been equally remarkable. The scale of the ship could only be appreciated in the final moments, as his ship manoeuvred from the perfectly circular creamy white rear, around to the perfectly black front, which was speckled with lit windows which provided a glimpse into the starships interior, and the tall flared tower of the single Potter-Onabule engine intake in the dead centre.

The rear was perfectly white, 500 metres across, and almost featureless apart from the dark 'well' which was the engine 'exhaust'. Once the ship moved out past Jupiter, its vast sails would open and almost double its diameter and eventually, many years from now, the actual engine would start to generate thrust as it streaked between the stars, accelerating ever faster.

The ship was the very peak of human engineering, and as such no expense had been spared. If this crew were to be away from home for the length of time the mission planners anticipated, then they were going to travel in luxury and style. This was no utilitarian vessel, the finishes were the finest materials available, and within the cabins and social spaces, the furniture was fabulous with rich deep wooden tables and luxurious fabric couches, designed to be both hard wearing and provide the greatest possible sense of aesthetic pleasure. The walls were made from a chromo-reactive material and could be set to any one of many millions of shades and colours, with many pre-programmed collections available for selection. Of course, all walls could also be utilised as screens, but this was generally discouraged apart from when part of a collective social activity, as addiction to permanent access to screens had long been known to be detrimental to mental health. The crew could call up pretty much any painting by any painter from the entire history of art, depicted in ultra-high definition, with suggestions based on the current preferences and colour schemes selected by the resident.

With a crew of just eighteen genetically modified astronauts, the ship was heading out towards Jupiter where it would leave the largely symbolic military escort behind and accelerate out towards Alpha Centuri, the Sun's nearest stellar neighbour (apart from Proxima Centuri, it's closely orbiting neighbour) and the best bet for detecting intelligent life. Sigur was leading the escort, and while he had been training for the mission for many years, this would only be the second time he had met the Captain.

Planning for the mission had been taking place for over four hundred years, with an enormous orbiting solar constellation of over one thousand stellar satellites constructed around the Sun designed to harvest remarkable amounts of energy from the star, before focussing it on one single enormous laser orbiting in a stable orbit some three hundred million miles from the sun. The laser had a single purpose; to provide power and propulsion to the starship during the initial phase of the 250 year (Earth time) journey, along with the breaking energy required to slow the ship when it returned home in two and a half centuries time.

However, while the engineering task was truly enormous, and required the construction of huge space stations at the various Lagrange points between the Earth, Mars , Venus and the Sun, as well as a number of asteroid mining facilities, it was not actually this that caused the project to require such long term strategic planning. It was in fact, the bio-engineering of the most extensively genetically modified people ever to have been created.

While the crew had been designed with a number of modifications to help them survive deep space, such as high resistance to radiation and almost total cellular stability which had never been observed to mutate throughout all the initial ground-based phases of the mission, it was the metabolic rate which was the most remarkable. The crew moved, talked, ate and aged at a rate so incredibly slowly, it was only possible to see it on stop motion camera. In fact, the ageing process was estimated to be some thirty times slower than standard and, even without the incredible cellular stability, they had an expected lifespan in excess of two thousand years. In fact, communication with the crew was managed through a highly specialist interface whereby crew members recorded messages over very long periods of time which were then played back at high speed to the scientists and engineers working on the mission. They also had a series of additional 'emergency' protocols which could be employed, which allowed them to act at higher speeds, but only in exceptional circumstances.

Captain Daniel Radisson had been fundamental to the mission and had stood out in the early stages of development as being extremely cognitive and able to demonstrate high levels of intuitive thinking which allowed for some acceleration of the process. He had also shown remarkable leadership when a number of the crew considered leaving the programme which led to a huge moral debate about how they had been created for such a singular function and it totally relied on them for success.

The Captain was now just over three hundred years old, and as such not much more than a teenager, but was already very aware and focussed on the mission he had been created to lead and understood his responsibilities. He had requested Admiral Sigur to join him in his quarters before the ship accelerated into the slingshot around Jupiter that would set them on their way to the stars; leaving the military escort behind to take a wider orbit, utilising Jupiters massive gravitational field to help propel them back to Earth. The message requesting the Admiral's company had, by all accounts, been started some months before, and the Admiral had been told that the Captain had started moving towards the couch in his lounge where he would meet the Admiral shortly after the HSS_2 left it's construction facility in orbit around Earth.

Although Sigur himself was a highly trained and genetically modified soldier and leader of the Special Astronaut Service, he could not help but have some trepidation in advance of the meeting. To meet such a super specialist Mod, who's design and development had started almost half a millennium ago, was nothing short of historic and would be remembered for many years to come. He clutched his gift, as is tradition, for the departing captain, very aware that should he ever make it back to Earth it would be many hundreds of years in the future at the very least. He (Sigur) would be long gone but hopefully mankind would remain. The gift he carried was a modified tablet, built to the most exacting standards, containing every book ever written by man, along with every piece of music ever composed (at least those for which there was still an existing recording and that had survived The Great Decline), but with the functionality to allow it to be slowed down many times so that it would make sense to the captain.

Sigur arrived at the Captain's quarters and as he approached the door it slid open and Sigur walked inside.

Chapter 7: Starmen

Joseph Onabule was born in a remote region of Africa, formerly known as Nigeria, in 2868AD, towards the end of The Great Decline. The youngest of five children he was a remarkable child who's piercing eyes and unusually dark skin was over-shadowed by his truly formidable intellect. By the age of three he could already read and write clearly, understood advanced mathematical concepts and effortlessly conversed with adults in a way that astonished everyone who came into contact with him. As he grew his intellect only became more remarkable and by the age twelve he had won a scholarship to the University of Lagos, one of the most esteemed universities still open in the world at the time.

His interest in mathematics developed alongside an intuitive intelligence about the natural world, which eventually led him into studying physics and chemistry. By the age of eighteen he moved to Mexico and the headquarters of NASA (which had long since disconnected itself from the fractured and failed states of North America) and continued to study while also working within the Theoretical Engineering team. Reportedly he was fairly unassuming at the time, but non of his colleagues doubted his intelligence and he was given lots of space to think and develop ideas. However, no one really realised the depth of his thinking and the ideas and mathematics he was starting to develop, and how he would eventually apply it to solving the problems which had stuck theoretical physics in a rut for hundreds of years.

This investment of time eventually paid off and Onabule published a paper that was to change everything and shepherd in a golden age of mankind – The Great Leap Forward.

His paper was the culmination of over a thousand years of intellectual endeavour, from Newton through James Clerk Maxwell to Albert Einstein and Max Planck (but which went woefully silent throughout The Great Decline) and finally reconciled all the theories of physics into one cohesive whole. It explained the elusive dark matter and dark energy and why it had been so difficult to detect, why gravity did not appear consistent with the quantum mechanics and why the value of 'G' (the gravitational constant, and in fact all the other natural constants, which he proved wasn't a constant at all, but slowly changing over time) had the value it had. It explained how quantum mechanics actually worked, how Quantum Entanglement appeared to transmit information at greater than light speed, and what was going on behind particle wave duality. It tied all these natural phenomena together into a beautiful if fiendishly complex whole.

His breakthrough was to recognise and develop the mathematics of the three distinct parts of spacetime (broadly speaking, The Future, The Present and The Past) and the boundaries between them, and connect them together through a series of transitional states. Describing the future as a multiverse of potential that actually exists (and always had), from the instant of the Big Bang, and a part of space time with its own set of remarkable particles, forces and properties – most of which had to be measured as negative values with the ability to travel faster than light until hitting The Present (or as Onabule put it, the Now Wave, which he described as a shock wave spreading out from the Big Band and the birth of the physical structure of the Universe). The Now Wave extended across not just a single 'Planck' moment, but very precisely seven transitional moments each of which represented a step in the process of the exotic future multiverse transforming into the absolute and fixed part of Spacetime we recognise as The Past. The present had by far the most complex set of mathematical relationships needed to describe the transitions between each of the distinct quantum moments.

It is in those seven moments that we play out our lives, that we perceive the flow of time and exist sandwiched ever so tightly within the Now Wave.

Onabule proved beyond doubt that The Past was truly rigid – in fact could a piece of even the softest substance once in the past be moved into the present it would prove to be several hundred times more rigid than the strongest diamond. Even a bubble of soap would require an almighty laser to break it's surface. This laid to rest once and for all the Grandfather paradox (where a grand-child goes back in time to kill his own grandfather before he himself had been conceived) and as Onabule himself explained, if it was possible to send a conscious mind back in time to kill a grandparent, all that would happen would be that the illusion of free will would be shattered as at no point would the mind be able to physically achieve the objective.

If the physics of the past was largely crystalline, but across four tightly bound dimensions, the physics of the future was incredibly fluid across many variable dimensions. It was here that the matter and force which was responsible for dark matter and dark energy actually existed, at least until the third moment of the Now Wave, by which point it had almost entirely evaporated away – dark matter becoming dark energy, which itself was almost immediately expended as it transferred into the kinetic energy of accelerated expansion of the universe; all of which explained why it was so elusive in the present. Onabule described how the influence of these forces on The Present were 'emergent' after most of it had in fact been obliterated in the firestorm of the leading edge of the Now Wave, which raced through spacetime, destroying almost all of this exotic matter as it rapidly condensed it into the past.

Again, as Onabule explained, just ahead of us (in time) was an Armageddon burning through everything, and we sat warming in the embers of a slush that rapidly turned to ice in an incredibly short space of time (around 60×10 to the power of -43).

While it took some time for other physicists and mathematicians to work through the equations and unique mathematical tools that Onabule had developed to extend across the dimensions, and start to unlock what it all meant; and what the new physics might allow for, one thing was very clear – the laws Einstein presented within Special Relativity remained intact and true. Breaking through the light speed barrier would never be possible and even travelling at close to light speed would create such temporal distortions that any interstellar traveller would return to Earth many years after departing, as time travels so much slower (relative to anyone not moving as fast) on a ship moving at these speeds.

This represented a huge barrier to any thoughts of interstellar empires and regular pan galactic travel at any imagined faster than light 'warp speed'. However, the impact on quantum mechanics and the ability to manipulate matter and therefore engineering of all sorts (including bio and computing), was transformative and so sparked the Great Leap Forward – the last great era of mankind.

Captain Daniel Radisson

Admiral Shadow walked into the cabin and sat in the chair directly opposite the Captain as the invite had requested. As he did so he saw the Captain's eyes widen ever so slightly and his breathing start to quicken as he initiated his 'Mid Pace Action Protocol'. As the Admiral waited he couldn't help but be impressed with the

Captain's physical presence. Every fibre of the man was a picture of almost total perfection and unimaginable strength. In some ways, the admiral thought to himself, he looked almost as if made from stone, with skin the texture of polished dark rose quartz, especially when operating at minimum metabolic speed.

He was aware of the process and watched as the Captain's internal systems jacked themselves up to approaching normal speed, with assistance from the additional electronic bionics he had embedded around his biological body.

While the Captain approached standard speed, the Admiral quickly glanced around the room, taking in the current colour scheme of the green of grass, fading up to the azure blue of a beautiful summers day on earth. There was tiny flecks of gold within the green, like buttercups dotted around a field, which gently swayed and faded in and out. It was incredibly serene and relaxing and instantly put the Admiral at ease.

The HSS2 crew were enhanced with electro-biomechanical systems, principally to support emergency and communications protocols which allowed them to act at a range of speeds. In fact, they could, when required, act and think at incredibly high speeds, far beyond those of a normal human, but these protocols were only to be utilised in exceptional circumstances, as they were considered to have a detrimental impact on their principle function, which was to live as long as is possible.

'Good morning Admiral' said the Captain with a wide smile. The rest of the Captain's body remained largely motionless, but the smile was warm, friendly and full of humour and confidence.

Remarkable for a man about to head off at speeds never before experienced by a human being, into the interstellar abyss in the direction of the nearest star with the prospect of life; Alpha Centauri – a mere 4.3 light years away, thought the Admiral.

'Good Morning Captain' replied the Admiral, returning the smile, but more out of respect than due to natural character. He had never seen this level of activation before and flattered that the Captain was expending so much of his resource on him.

'I have to thank you for the escort Admiral – I know it is largely symbolic, but it has been re-assuring to know your Corps has been at our sides while we complete this initial stage of our journey'

'Of course Captain – it has been an honour to be part of such a historic mission, even if only as a supporting actor'.

'Ah, your modesty becomes you Admiral, we both know that for a while both our names will be celebrated in the history books' The Captain's grin widened and the Admiral felt that he knew something but wasn't saying.

'Well, you will at least get the privilege of returning to read whatever was written in the history books long after the authors who wrote them, and I, have long passed!'

'Perhaps' laughed the Captain 'There is certainly many, many miles to cover, and a great deal of time, before that could become true, but let us see – time will undoubtedly tell.' The Captain hesitated for a moment.

'Anyway, it is, I am told, a custom to present a gift to the accompanying senior officer on such missions; and I have given considerable time, and some expense I might say, on yours. I am told you are a keen listener of the 20th century music known as jazz'.

'I am' replied the Admiral – and he was, but once he had confessed this publicly he almost always received gifts of antique recordings, of which he already had many, and as soon as he heard this his heart sank – well at least his gift would look pretty good in comparison!

The Captain smiled again 'And I believe you are soon to retire'

'Also correct' said Sigur 'You have been doing your research'

'Well if you don't mind, as I have not been permitted to activate my full motion protocols, and I don't want to be upsetting the Crew Engineers this early in the mission by disobeying a direct order, if you could please look behind the sofa you will find two cases. I would be very grateful if you could bring them over and open them up for me'.

The Admiral walked over to the sofa and was mildly surprised to see one quite large case, and a second looking rather like a briefcase. He brought the cases back to the low table.

'If you could please open the larger of the two cases' said the Captain, still smiling (Of course, noted Shadow, he is actually still very young).

Admiral Shadow flicked the latches and opened the case and to his astonishment discovered a beautifully crafted tenor saxophone inside, but unlike any he had seen in the history books, it was completely coated in Vantablack – the deepest and darkest pigment ever created by mankind. It was a truly beautiful thing and the Admiral was genuinely taken aback.

'Why, thank you Captain – I am really surprised. I don't play but I always intended learning some musical instrument or other once retired, but this is really exceptional'. The Admiral had not even seen a real saxophone, never mind played one, so this really was out of the ordinary.

'The alloy is almost indestructible and modelled exactly from a Selmer Mk 6 – apparently the best sax ever made, so you will be able to take into any conflict zone! If you look in the other case, you will find a tuition book and a copy of The Great American Songbook- both made of the same material'.

The Admiral was taken aback – his tablet now looked a bit weak in comparison, he thought rather ruefully, but still, what an amazing gift…

The two men conversed a little longer, Admiral Shadow presented his gift and encouraged the Captain to explore the music of the late 20th Century, and Daniel asked about how he became interested in jazz in the first place. Shadow explained it had been by chance – just a meeting in a bar a long time ago in New New York with a stranger who was already fanatical about jazz and the history of New York City and what it must have been like back in the 20th Century.

Talking to the Captain was easy; a natural meeting of two similar people, highly modified specialists, but still very human. Suddenly a quiet alarm sounded, indicating that the strictly timed protocol was soon to expire and it was time for the meeting to end. Admiral Shadow stood and turned to leave, picking up his gifts on the way as Captain Daniel Radisson returned to his ultra slow state and his smile froze. 'I am never going to forget this meeting' he said to himself as he walked off down the corridor, feeling for all the world like a kid who had just been given the best birthday present ever.

Chapter 8: Oh Danny Boy, The Pipes are Calling. (1945AD)

Little Danny Ryan rushed through the noisy streets, climbing the short hill as groups of people stood outside the pubs singing and laughing and rejoicing the news that following Hitler's death in the last week, the Nazi's had finally surrendered. The evenings were getting lighter and warmer, and even though tonight was a little overcast, no one cared. After five miserable years, the war was finally over. However, despite the occasion, it was not what was on Danny's mind.

He cut up an alleyway, pulling his over-size standard issue US army trench coat around him and keeping his head down as he worked his way through the crowds milling around the edge of the market square. Many of the revellers were already a little worse for wear and several tried to pull him into the celebrations, but while he smiled and shook the occasional hand, he did not stop or let his pace slow down. He had an important mission to complete and would be working throughout the night. He kept a firm grip on his bag and headed over to the far corner of the market, before turning down Foundry Lane and then an immediate left onto Oak Street and alongside The George and Dragon, known amongst the locals as Band on the Wall – his final destination.

As soon as he arrived at the corner door he ducked inside, past yet more people celebrating and into the heavy throng of the very busy pub. He could hear the music being played by the band, peculiarly perched up on a stage suspended from the far wall with customers directly underneath (hence the name) – Danny smiled, he had been here so many times before but it never failed to amuse him.

He went over to the bar.

'Hi Ernie – I'm here' he called to the Landlord ' you need some taps fixing?

'Hiya Danny – still working, even tonight' replied the burley landlord, 'I wasn't expecting you to be honest – It's a big day Danny, sometimes it's important to celebrate' said the landlord with the familiar Irish twang to his accent 'I have even booked a chap to come in tomorrow and take some photographs – he has a proper camera, a really top quality one, ye know, like the newspapers use...'

Danny smiled back 'I'll have to come over and make sure I get into the photo' Even though Danny was only in Manchester temporarily, he had already picked up jobs as a plumber around the city as there was such a huge shortage of decent tradesmen. Of course this was just a cover, but it worked well and gave Danny the access he was looking for.

He headed off to the stairs to the cellar with his bag over his shoulder. He had actually almost finished the job and this would be his last visit – a shame, he really liked the place, the music, the people and the whole atmosphere. Not surprising, in various forms it had taken him over one hundred years to build it, commissioning the early structure, convincing the architects to build the metal frame around the outside of the building, with what looked like stone columns actually cast from incredibly pure iron which would remain standing for thousands of years. It had raised eyebrows but as long as he was paying he got his way, and he had been careful to break the contracts up over many years and to build the place in stages; slowly expanding from the original footprint.

So tonight he was about to fix some of the final pieces of electronics, deeply embedded into the structure of the building. Directly under the stage, was a machine that no one from the twentieth century would recognise at all. In fact it would be almost a thousand years before another human being would even be able to make a guess at what it was, and several thousand before anyone else would be able to construct anything like it. It was still fiendishly complex thing to set up and it would no doubt take most of the night, but once wired into the rest of the hidden machinery embedded throughout the building, it would be encased in an almost impenetrable casket and left for another ten thousand years when it would finally be taken out of standby and fulfil it's function, along with the rest of the almost completely indestructible building. It would be another eighty years or so before the next element of the machine was to be added as a large extension to the building would be built on. An extensive metal frame, which was actually a huge transmitter arial, would be installed into what was now (in 1945) the adjacent fruit and veg wholesaler. Created supposedly as a frame to prop up the ageing facade, the complex design would have to be connected into the machinery Danny was installing on this long spring night here in 1945, early in the twenty first century, around the time of the first great pandemic.

Danny worked through the night, ignoring the sound of celebrations coming from the streets around him. He could hear Ernie singing upstairs until the early hours when things finally quietened down. Eventually, around 9am, he was done, the machine was primed and tested and he stood up and stretched his back. He picked up his jacket and headed off up the stairs, 'Time for a beer I think' he said to himself quietly as he stepped through the door at the top of the cellar stairs and into the sunlight streaming through the windows on the side of the building.

Mathew Tyson, Ernie's brother, was there, holding court and directing people to spread out, get drinks and take their seats, as was Ernie's daughter, but Ernie himself was nowhere to be seen – probably nursing the mother of all hangovers. Over by the bar, opposite the stage, stood a great tripod with a camera perched on top. It made Danny smile, it was the opposite end of the technology spectrum to the device he had just installed in the cellar and in many ways represented the start of the journey that man would take over the next few thousand years in understanding the nature of light and information and what that all would come to mean. Once he had managed to get a beer Danny walked over to a table in the middle of the crowd. He knew where he would sit and despite the pub being packed, his seat remained empty, waiting for his inevitable arrival. He sat down, nodded a hello to the other soldiers sat there, took a sip of his beer, straightened his beret and glasses, and with a enigmatic smile, turned and looked directly into the camera just as the flash went off.

The HSS2 or **Hyper Speed Startship 2**, to give it its full title, was the most remarkable machine ever created by man. In fact it was an assembly of a number of jaw dropping machines, each and all representing the absolute pinnacle of human engineering and ingenuity. Designed to move up to twenty people across interstellar space, the whole project had taken almost four hundred years to fully develop, not least to create the Mod crew, including the ethical and legal challenges, but most of all the raw engineering, both mechanical and biological.

The ship itself looked for all the world like an enormous upside down mushroom; (white on top and black underneath) or a flying saucer like the UFO's of 20th century urban legend, but with a tall elegant conical and perfectly circular tower extended from the top (the stem of the mushroom) and a large dark hole on the opposite side of the disk. The direction of travel was to fly 'stem first' and the side facing the stars was painted in pure Vantablack, with dots of light scattered across the surface where windows allowed the crew to look out at the stars. The side facing back towards the sun, was in contrast, the 'whitest white' (White 9.99), which also created a surface which was difficult to focus on and gave the impression of a perfectly smooth blob of ice cream floating against the backdrop of the cosmos.

It also had a huge circular sail which almost doubled the ships overall circumference, and reflected the colour scheme of the main body of the ship.

However, there were very precise reasons for it's shape and colour it had nothing to do with the romance of the past.

While the ship carried hydrogen tanks which were to be used for the initial exit from Earth orbit and a burst of speed around Jupiter, (which could also be re-charged through the collection of free hydrogen gas as it entered and orbited the destination star), it was the ships other two propulsion systems that set it apart from anything else previously built.

The ship had been designed by teams spread across the planet and involved many of the greatest minds of the day, many of whom applied their entire lifetimes to solving the various technical challenges. The whole thing had to be put together in orbit, as it would be far too large to launch from Earth's surface as an entirely pre-constructed space craft. It required an entire infrastructure of supply ships, industrial construction units and teams of astronaut engineers to piece the various bits together.

Of course, by definition, the HSS2 was not the only ship required by the mission – HSS1's construction timeline began some fifty years prior to it's successor and was an unmanned and fully automated version which was not only the test and trailblazer, but also an essential part of the return strategy for the HSS2.

This was because the HSS class starships were, at least for a significant part of the journey, effectively sailing ships, powered by an enormous array of solar collectors orbiting the sun, centralised around an extraordinarily high-powered precision engineered laser, which fired a truly frightening amount of energy at the receding ship, which then rode the beam with it's own set of enormous sails and perfectly circular base. The ship also drew significant power from the laser for it's own internal workings and to initially 'charge' the next stage propulsion system.

This had to be, at least to some extent, replicated for the return journey, and while building a full array would not be possible, the **HHS1** would have some years to distribute it's own solar collectors around Alpha Centauri and charge it's internal Potter-Onabule engine which could then power the laser which made up the bulk of it's payload. The laser itself would also provide the final 'break' to slow the **HSS2** down as it entered Alpha Centauri's orbit, which would still be travelling at a break neck speed, but once the 'laser brake' from the HSS1 had managed to slow the HSS2 enough, it would be tight and slow enough to be captured by the stars gravitational field.

The HSS1 itself travelled significantly slower than the HSS2 so as to be able to be caught by the stars gravitational field without any additional braking – hence the extraordinarily large time gap between the launch of the two ships.

The point of the laser beyond anything else, was for the initial phase of the journey (both out and return) the ship required a constant acceleration at just under 0.25G, for some twenty years if it was to cross the void between the two stars. The total return voyage was in fact, around seventy years 'ship time' and almost ninety years 'Earth time', due to the time dilation effect of travelling at a significant proportion of light speed during the central part of the journey.

It was at this stage, when even the power of the laser had really dropped away, that the third, and truly mind-boggling, stage propulsion system kicked in.

The challenge for the design team was to provide propulsion without taking propellant on the journey, which would require vast tanks. This meant that the ship had to either be delivered it (as per the laser sending photons and pushing against the sales) or collect it along the way. And the only thing available (according to Onabule's calculations), existed ever so briefly in the first slices of time after the Now Wave and rapidly evaporated away into dark energy - the elusive substance known as dark matter. While scientists had spent hundreds of years searching for it in the post Einstein era, it was not until Onabule's calculations were developed that it was realised that dark matter was not stable and could not exist in 'present' or 'past' space time for anything other than the very first moments of the Now Wave, just enough time to make its presence known through the force of gravity.

Effectively what the engineers created was a dark matter jet propulsion engine which drew in mass from the dark matter ether. The drawback with the design was that it only worked once the ship had already reached a considerable velocity and the engine was spinning at truly astronomical speeds and fast enough to draw in dark matter at a high enough relative velocity for the engine to work.

The engine itself was an incredibly complex nuclear fusion reactor which also housed a proton 'turbine' which, once fully up to power, rotated at almost relativistic speeds, achieved by drawing energy from the laser from the outset of the journey and constantly increasing spin speed.

Once up to speed the engine was fuelled by a mix of tritium and deuterium (isotopes of Hydrogen), carried on board but also replenished from space as the ship swept along, which drove the fusion reaction taking place within the engine itself.

The engine was a donut shaped 'Torus' design and suspended within a superconducting magnetic ring sat at the front and dead centre of the ship. While the field that caused the rotation was electromagnetic and also created a deflecting vortex which extended many thousands of miles in front of the ship, the field that drew in and expelled the dark matter was something different entirely. Based around Onabule's multi-dimensional versions of Clerk's electromagnetic wave equations, but largely in reverse, it created a plasma of positrons, mathematically behaving like electrons travelling faster than light, and therefore, paradoxically and very briefly, backwards in time within the confines of the Now Wave.

While Dark Matter did not normally feel the forces of regular matter, or make its presence know other than through gravity, it reacted to the rapidly spinning positron vortex which sucked it into the compression chamber, creating a dark matter cyclone within the positron field which extended out in front of the ship, before finally sucking it into the engine, accelerating it and squeezing it out of the 'exhaust' on the bottom side of the ship, generating steady thrust.

Of course, the stresses this created were truly enormous, not least the power of the centrifugal force acting within the spinning turbine on the overall structure. Engineers overcame this by creating the sub-atomic shell which formed inside the turbine once it was spinning at enormous speeds. By utilising the strong nuclear force to create what was an incredibly thin but unbelievably strong crystal matrix of sub-atomic material containing a repeating shell of pure quarks, similar to the surface of a neutron star, or a single massive atom, and an almost impenetrable and indestructible structure.

The ship represented several thousands of years of human thinking and astonishing engineering innovation but once built every millimetre represented perfection; a truly beautiful and remarkable machine which would ultimately be the greatest thing ever made by mankind and would finally put at least the nearest stars within reach. However, as the programme developed and the years turned into decades and finally centuries, and the costs mounted way beyond all initial estimates, it was clear to pretty much everybody that the challenge of moving humans between the stars would never become routine. It was also clear, that as no verifiable signals or signs appeared from other alien civilisations, that this was probably the case for all life across the Galaxy, no matter how long they had been around for.

Chapter 9: God Bless the Chill

The band walked through the back stage and followed the stairs down into the dressing room before pulling a few beverages from the fridge and collapsing onto the sofas.

'Wow, what a show and...what a sound' said Georgia.

This in itself was amazing, and while no one said it, for Georgia to talk about the show as a whole, rather than her performance in particular, was extremely rare, never mind being complementary about the sound.

Red took a deep pull on her LPG vape, flames curling around her lips and out through her nostrils, before taking a deep swig of beer to dowse the flames.

'Yep, that really was something else – the crowd loved it' she said 'let's hope it's reflected in the bar sales' she followed up quietly and directed at Swan.

Chill, Kato and Georgia started up their own conversation around how clear the monitors were and what an amazing sound they got and why wasn't it like that every night as Red moved closer to Shadow.

'Well, we appear to have found ourselves another remarkable Natural to join the team' she said 'good to know we have options other than Archold'.

'Uh' he replied not really listening 'yes, absolutely – did you see the glow coming from my sax?' he said, instantly changing the subject 'Georgia said she saw something and now I think about it the whole thing felt a bit strange – almost like it was playing itself'

'Hhmm – maybe slightly self-absorbed there my dear' replied Red 'You played great, the band played great, it sounded great – it was just one of those nights that come along every now and then when everything falls into place'.

'Yes I know – but don't you think it's a bit odd that Danny arrives out of nowhere and on his very first night we basically have our best ever gig.? I know it may just be the uncertainty of having a new engineer when we have only ever known Archold…but also the sax glowing, I mean, it's made of Vantablack and vantablack definitely don't glow' he said, his black eyes glinting in his completely black face just enough for Red to tell he was frowning and his senses were heightened.

Red knew Shadow well enough to know that his military super senses were kicking in and that his enhanced intuitions should never be ignored out of hand.

'He said he had heard Georgia play before – do you ever remember him previously visiting the club?' he said quietly 'I'm sure we would have remembered wouldn't we..?'

Just at that moment Valentine came crashing into the room 'Have we got any more of the Ukrainian Malt Whisky? I have a queue from the bar to the stage and everyone is spending! Any chance of a hand?'

The two club owners jumped to their feet – the reality of running a venue taking over, and headed out of the door to help the staff max out the sales and keep the punters happy. Red headed over to the bar to help out and maintain some discipline, while Shadow headed for the cellar to get another case of the very fashionable, and expensive, Malt.

He called another quick thanks to the guys before heading around the corner and along the corridor towards the front of the building and the drinks cellar. The system of voice and iris recognition was difficult for Shadow, as his eye was almost entirely featureless, and so he carried a false eye on a bracelet on his wrist. Somewhat disconcerting to people who did not know why, especially as the eyeball was so realistic, but essential for Shadow to move around the building.

He entered the cellar, making sure he pulled the door closed behind him and flicked on the light, just in time to see the door leading to the sub stage pull shut at the far end of the cellar. It was only the last centimetre but he was sure he had seen it close, and he had learnt to always trust his super alert and highly trained senses. He walked towards the door and pulled the handle but it was locked just as it should be. He pulled out his eyeball again and commanded the door to open before hearing the click of the lock and pulled once again. This time it slid open and he stooped before climbing through into the void under the venue which stretched almost the full length of the old building, almost to the front of the stage.

He flicked on the light and looked around. There was no one there and everything was pretty much as it had been when he last came down here – which is to say, largely piled high with junk, some of which dated back to when the building was the renegade mutant HQ, and even before that as far as he knew. He had a quick look behind the nearest piles but he could already tell that there was no one in the room and the only noise was coming from the drinkers upstairs along with the beat of the tunes being played by the after show DJ. He went back into the beer cellar where he could hear voices and his name being called – he spun around on his heel and went back out the way he had come in. In fact it is the only way out so either someone was still in the sub stage or he had been mistaken. Easy to find out as he double locked the door from the outside before acknowledging Valentine who had loaded up with two cases of the finest Malt Whisky.

'I'll bring the beers' said Shadow as he picked up two cases under one arm, before grabbing another case of the malt.

———————————————

Shadow pushed his way through the crowd, the room was dark and noisy, so he was almost completely invisible, but the regulars recognised him as he glided through the darkness and several compliments came his way, to which he nodded and replied with a few terse 'thanks' . Red was busy remonstrating the bar staff while joking with the punters and simultaneously pouring multiple drinks when Shadow arrived with his supplies.

'Here you go' he said as he effortlessly hefted them onto the bar.

'Better late than never' replied Red, without breaking her stride for a moment 'can you check everything is ok in the venue – not sure if I heard a bit of an argument going on'

Shadow turned around and headed back into the main venue just in time to see the house lights come up to 50% as Vivian, the very tiny doorman, was starting to square up to a mutant at least three times his size. Shadow walked towards the pair and as he did so, just on the other side, he saw Danny walk out of the back stage area carrying some cables he was idly wrapping up. However it was not the cable that caught Shadow's attention, but the dust on the back of his head which he was casually brushing away. The sight was logged and parked in Shadow's brain while he continued to deal with the issue immediately in front of him.

'What's up Viv' said Shadow casually.

'This dude – says he wants his money back – doesn't like jazz'. The last part Vivian said in a very hushed voice as if swearing in church…

Shadow invisibly, but visibly, coiled into his deep passive aggressive mode before asking ever so quietly.

'Hhhmmm…and when did you decide you didn't like jazz – before, during or after the gig?'

The reaction whenever anyone realised that Shadow was the club owner, especially when being difficult, was always the same… somewhat like a canoeist realising they had inadvertently paddled headlong towards a deadly waterfall and that they needed to start back-pedalling immediately and with all their might. It did not matter how big the adversary, it was just not going to be worth the hassle of taking on Shadow in his own space.

What non of them realised was that it was actually Vivian they should be most concerned about. Genetically modified to de-commission nuclear plants, he was almost indestructible, pretty strong and with a stamina that meant he just never stopped – either talking, arguing or if it really came to it, dragging undesirables from the club.

The mutant rapidly denied saying any such thing, and clarified that he was 'only just learning to like jazz' and tonight 'had been a real revelation' and 'could Shadow possibly recommend any particular recordings to help educate his musical ear'

Only half concentrating, Shadow started to list a number of classic jazz records he knew was available on the Modbook playlists, but really he was thinking about Danny, who he was and what he had been doing. Just at that moment, Chill stepped in and started casually chatting with the guy, expanding on Shadow's suggestions and providing background on the tracks. He was great like that and could always calm down any miscreant and lighten the mood. Shadow smiled to himself, they will no doubt be best of friends by the end of the night and the guy will probably turn into a regular.

Chapter 10 The Fast and the Slow (3848 AD - relative Earth time)

The Captain moved purposefully down the corridor of HSS2 – most of the rest of the crew were fast asleep after the remarkable events of the last few weeks when they had finally turned on the Onabule-Potter Dark Matter Cyclone engine, generating actual thrust from the dark matter cloud they were passing through.. It had actually been on for the whole 20 year flight, steadily drawing energy from the laser directed from earth, building up rotational momentum and priming itself for the initiation of drive mode.

The Captain had very carefully overseen the entire process, working alongside the Chief Engineer to make sure that the pulses of energy entering the fusion reactor had exactly the expected effect before moving onto the next phase of the process. But now, quietly and secretly, he needed to initiate one last adjustment to the engine systems to provide just one tiny additional boost of energy and ultimately to change the ships destination.

A lot rested on him getting it exactly right – in fact a series of unfolding events across the entirety of space-time – but he was used to that kind of pressure and had spent a very, very long time preparing for it, one way or another. So, undeterred, he hurried on to the bridge. Of course, hurrying on board HS2 had a very different meaning to back on Earth, he had set his clock a good four hours early giving himself plenty of time to travel the 150 meters or so to the ships Bridge so he did not have to initiate any emergency protocols and attract any unwanted attention. But in the slow motion world of HSS2, he moved with intent and purpose, knowing exactly what he needed to achieve and how long he had to get the job done.

The tolerances within the Potter-Onabule Engine were literally atomic scale and the designers knew the exact mass to a single atom of each component. Based on Onabule's original equations, to operate fully it needed to already be spinning at fantastic speeds, while also travelling at a considerable velocity through the dark matter 'ether' perpendicular to the direction of travel.

Often counter intuitive to brains used to flying craft being aero-dynamic, the HSS2 flew 'flat' against the direction of travel, with the 'intake' of the single engine situated in the dead centre around which was essentially an immensely powerful particle accelerator generating a huge electro-magnetic field. When commissioned on Earth the engine contained a cloud of protons which the machine had steadily accelerated over the initial years of the mission.

Once spinning fast enough and through the extreme centrifugal forces inside the engine, this cloud eventually began to squeeze together to form a dense shell of matter, eventually being forced into such close proximity it began to move into the realms of Onabule's equations, and outside of the old standard model.

However, the formation of the shell was purely a step in the process and had largely been achieved while still still relatively close to the Sun. It was the acceleration of that shell to almost light speed which had taken the time, and required the ship itself to be moving at a significant proportion of the speed of light itself. Achieved by harnessing the power of the sun and powering the ship for 20 years or so (ship time) by the incredible laser built by another team of engineers, delivering constant power and a steady rate of acceleration of around 0.25G's, providing the crew with a constant, if much reduced relative to earth, illusion of gravity.

Hovering between quantum states as fundamental particles start to jump in and out of existence, the engine generated a Gravitational Wave vortex which travelled at light speed in front of the ship. This field began to interact with the rapidly evaporating dark matter cloud which existed very briefly at the back end of the Now Wave – the smoke from the firestorm of creation, accelerating it towards the engine intake manifold while still far ahead of the ship, before dragging it through the engine and ejecting it out of the rear of the ship to generate thrust.

Once the HSS2 had left Earth's orbit and the shell continued to accelerate over the initial phase of the journey, it eventually achieved a rotational velocity of almost 90% the speed of light and at the same time the ship was travelling, relative to the Earth, at almost 9% of the speed of light, providing a vector velocity of almost light speed and at which point General Relativity effects also kicked in as it began to increase in relative mass and create it's own gravitational field. Through the effect of the cyclonic vortex, reached out ahead of the ship, sucking in dark matter created by Tachyons, a form of matter which moved faster than light speed, hitting the Now Wave and condensing, ever so briefly, into positive 'dark' matter before it evaporated away into Dark Energy. As the cyclone entered the engine, the pressure of negative energy produced as the exotic matter started to convert into the repulsive dark energy had the potential to generate vast amounts of thrust.

The machine also collected all normal (if extremely diffuse) matter and funnelled that through the same central intake of the engine, not only providing thrust (according to the more straight forward Newton's laws of Motion), but also protecting the ship from any impacts when travelling at such high speeds.

The ship could easily accelerate up to three or four G's in an emergency, but when already travelling at remarkable speeds it would rapidly come up against the limitations described in Einstein's Special Theory of Relativity increasing the time dilation relative to the Earth or any other much slower moving object, and that was already something that the mission planners and politicians had to struggle with.

This was, in many ways, the real challenge- interstellar travel was possible and an engine that could provide the thrust was also possible –

it jumped out of Onabule's calculations and theory and was recognised by the great man himself, but stopping and starting would always take such a significant amount of time and energy, and the effects of time dilation (as time slowed to almost nothing relative to Earth as velocity increased), it was just so annoyingly impractical. Once the ship dropped below a certain speed, for instance to drop into orbit around a star, the energy required to re-accelerate always had to come from an external source and the amount of time passed back at home, compared to the on-board ship time, meant that any travellers would come back to a world that had completely changed, with generations come and gone and non of the mission team who initiated the programme, or friends and families, politicians or world leaders, still alive to greet them.

So early on in the planning it became clear that creatures evolving within a normal macro time scale could not crew such vessels. The crew had to be made, created in the lab, built to psychologically withstand huge timescales with nothing to do, that in fact lived within a completely different time frame and only really related to each other. They had to be super survivors, extraordinarily resilient and intelligent; and without any real links or concept of 'home', but principally with metabolic rates so slow that to normal humans they would barely appear to be alive at all.

This still did not deal with the need for an interstellar infrastructure of booster stations which would provide the 'jump start' the ships needed to operate effectively, and so the idea of moving the ships in pairs began to formulated, sending an advance vessel out to a star to start the process of 'charging' the Onabule engine prior to the second ships arrival, taking with it the sun energy harvester and laser booster needed to re-accelerate the second ship back out of the system, leapfrogging between stars as it did so.

Or so that was the plan, but unfortunately bigger and greater plans were afoot, thought through in even greater detail, developed over millennia and unfolding like clockwork.

These were all things that Captain Radisson understood implicitly, he also realised that the planets around Alpha Centauri were relatively uninteresting balls of mud or gas and to drop back below the engine's operational speed would be a waste of the time, effort and energy required to get them to this point. In fact Captain Radisson knew a whole lot more than most realised; he also understood that the genetic engineers who had created him had done a far better job than they thought and that, while not actually immortal, his lifespan would be far far longer than they had projected. He also knew that planets bearing life, especially intelligent life, especially what we might describe as advanced, civilised life was far far far more unusual and improbable than any of the first speculations of alien civilisations had initially envisaged (admittedly, after years of searching, many other scientists were beginning to reach the same conclusion). But most of all that the Earth, even in the damaged state it had been in prior to The Great Leap Forward, was a remarkable diamond in the rough, a one in a trillion, trillion phenomena, an oasis to be cherished and persevered. What no one else truly understood, however, was that these diamonds were an essential, if extremely rare, component in a stable Universe.

Chapter II: The Greatest Mind (2896 AD)

Professor Onabule sat back into his chair and stared at his computer screen. The last pieces of the puzzle were finally falling into place, the symmetry in the equations emerging as his new theory predicted. Out with the old 'Standard Model' of particle physics, and in with his new multi-dimensional model, sub-dividing space time and resolving the discrepancy with gravity and all the other contradictions with Einstein's relativity. In its place he had built a whole new suite of particles which existed, and were bound by, the various regions and transitional dynamics of space time. The new family contained well over one hundred different particles, expanded from the three groups already described and found within the Standard Model, but brought in an additional seven subdivisions. The mathematics was fiendishly complex, but he had been working on it for so long he could now rotate the whole model around in his mind, testing the theory from all directions and doing massive multiple simultaneous calculations.

However, like so many other previous theories, he was still perplexed by the ability to test the theory through experimentation. The challenges that any experimenter would have to overcome would be formidable, and while he had a world class engineers background, even he struggled to imagine how any experiment could be set up to operate at the very leading edge of his 'Now Wave' interacting with the particles in the very earliest moments of that part of space time before they evaporated away leaving only the non virtual particles that could be found on Earth and which were detectable in the here and now.

He leant back on his chair, looked out at the blistering sun dropping low over the high rise Mexico City skyline and beaming through his 23rd floor window of the Feynman Building, the headquarters of NASA, and let his mind wander, listening to colossal saxophone of John Coltrane weaving through the chords on his antique record player.

His mind was already wandering through the permutations of criticism that would be levelled at his work; anticipating the peer reviews and myriad of proofs that he had already worked through and detailed reposts to the challenges he had already constructed for himself. It wasn't lost on him that the way his mind worked was not dissimilar to those of a quantum computer... or of 20th Century jazz performer for that matter, and he made a note to himself to pursue this intellectual enquiry at some point in the future.

Just then, there was a knock at the door. He looked up, somewhat startled – no one ever came up here to his office, certainly not at this time of the evening, and if they did they tended to avoid him. He understood his reputation of being unforgiving of fools, and relatively speaking, pretty much everyone else was one, so they tended to keep their distance, which suited him just fine. He looked over at the door, and projected his voice, emphasising his African accent, which he also found intimidated people 'come in'. The door opened and in walked a rather diminutive young European woman with dark hair and round black glasses. 'Good Evening Professor Onabule' she said, 'I am Dr Daniella Potter, from the charged particles engineering team, and I have been working on some ideas around how to create a high speed plasma vortex using protons within a fusion reactor and wondered if you could help me with some of the calculations...'

Onabule's eyes widened, and a multitude of thought pathways passed through his mind. 'Of course...Daniella, a very interesting problem – I would be happy to, please send me over your files' he said in an uncharacteristically quiet and polite tone 'Of course' he said again to himself...

Chapter 12: The Room

Shadow was instantly awake, in fact he did not have a 'dozing' mode; he was pretty much either off or on. He rolled over, away from Red, pivoting his lower body out of the bed adjusting his balance and using the weight of his legs to spin his body into an upright position. His blackness disguising the incredibly smooth movement in the dark of the bedroom at the top of the club.

Last night's gig was remarkable, just the best they had ever played together as a unit and for the first time he really felt as if they were reaching the peaks of some of the 20th Century jazz greats. However, he just could not shake the feeling that something was going on with

Danny. It was his training, the intuitive matrices designed into his brain by the original genetic engineers who had created the first battalions of Shadow Core soldiers. He had learned to trust it, it might be a minor thing, but there was definitely something that just did not ring true with their new engineer.

Of course, he was busy and always had things to do, but this was nagging at him, so he logged it and took it upon himself to keep him close, under surveillance, and just check whether there really was another motive at work with the Natural Human engineer. In the meantime, things to do, so he continued to move and stood up and strode off towards the bathroom, glancing back as Red began to stir, one long slender leg exposed across the bed sheets.

The first few days of the week were always busy – even though audience numbers dropped, preparing for another busy weekend always meant that there was plenty to do, and this took Shadow's mind off any concerns he had with Danny. Georgia would do the Monday as a Trio with Chill and Kato, and Red had booked another local band to cover a couple of nights, just to give them a chance to catch up, but word had definitely spread about last weekend's show and most enquiries for tickets were asking about when the My Funny Quarantine band would be back on stage again.

Soon enough, it was Friday, and the full band line-up was due to appear. Shadow, and in fact all the band, were feeling the need to play again and the soundcheck already felt pretty buzzy, with everyone pushing each other and breaking out of their normal patterns. Improvisation was like that, Shadow never ceased to be amazed at how instantaneously everyone in the band could jump onto new patterns and riffs, almost as if the communication was instantaneous. Of course, he was engineered to have lightning speed reactions, but this was something else, beyond the speed of thought and, being honest with himself, it was Georgia who was most intuitive and could pick up on a new 'lick' or rhythm when it first emerged in any one of the other players, building it into a whole new part of the tune and taking all the rest of the band into a different musical place. Sometimes loud, sometimes quiet, but always unexpected and exciting.

Everything was checked and working just as it should when Shadow once again spotted Danny slipping away towards the stairs and the cellar, and again his senses began tingling. Without making any sudden changes in position, he refocussed his hearing to extend beyond his vision, carefully logging the sounds that he could hear from the direction Danny had headed in. He noted he had left some cables on the side, and already had an armful of gear, so he probably meant to return. Without hesitation, Shadow strode off towards the stairs, bounded down them and slid into the cleaners cupboard just around the corner from the entrance to the cellar, pulling the door closed with his finger tips and listening out for the sound of the cellar door. Seconds passed before he heard it click again, followed by the light footsteps of Danny heading back up the stairs. Shadow counted the exact number of steps and as soon as he reached the top step, Shadow moved; he knew he had maybe three seconds to get to the door, open it and close it again before Danny picked up the leads and came back down. Easy for a man of Shadows skills, he crossed the corridor, put his eyeball lock against the pad, pulled the door open and closed all in one incredibly rapid and smooth movement. Once inside he headed to the door to the disused under-stage at the back of the cellar, and once inside slid into the dark shadows at the back, behind the ancient piles of stones that still lay on the equally ancient stone floor. He flattened himself to the wall and slowed his breathing and waited.

It didn't take long before he heard the click of the door, and Danny came walking through the space, quickly and confidently straight towards the far wall, carrying his bunch of cables. He dodged around the pillars holding up the stage and went into the corner, facing the wall and reaching out a hand to place on a brick at his exact shoulder height, and instantly a door opened up immediately in front of him. Shadow could see dim lights, like the glow of instrument panels and monitor screens, over Danny's shoulder, but without hesitation Danny walked through and entered the room beyond, turning to initiate the mechanism to close the door behind him, and as he did so looked straight into Shadow's face. Danny froze and Shadow stepped forward into the light. Whatever was going on there was really no point trying to hide it now. Danny lowered his arm.

'Well now, Mr Shadow, it was inevitable really... obviously I guessed you would catch me at some point, I just wanted a little more time before you did!' said Danny, a smile spreading across his lips. 'I guess you will be wanting an explanation now, but perhaps if we can wait until after the show? I assure you that I am not doing anything malicious...or illegal actually, in fact it's generally all for the good...of mankind, and, well, the club actually, and you...'

Shadow walked over 'Show me inside the room'. he said

Danny looked at his feet, and shuffled a bit.

'Of course' he said, stepping aside.

Chapter 13 : Mexico City (379 AD)

Admiral Sigur Shadow walked out of the subway station and out into the chaos and noise of the Tech Quarter of Mexico City, warm rain gushed down the slightly inclined street as the heavens bulged with muscular dark grey clouds. The area itself was a vibrant hub for the many tech artisans who had populated the quarter over the last few centuries; small units and larger engineering sheds spread through a random and bewildering maze of streets and alleyways heading in all directions. Neon lights stood proud of the shop fronts and projected holographs filled the air, and high powered laser projections etched the names of some of the larger engineering companies on the clouds overhead, animated to describe the services offered like immense bulging advertising boards. The impact of it all was overwhelming, with lights and noise in all directions, not at all diluted by the heavy and relentless rain.

The area began to grow at the very beginning of The GLF, fed by the students and other brilliant creatives who had flocked to the City's University and to work for the new Global Board and Executive which had replaced Earth's old style governments. Many of these began to organise themselves into collectives, or work for independent engineering and electronics firms, utilising the new advances in quantum computing and advanced 3D molecular alloy printing to design the tools required to be able to create all sorts of tech almost to order, delivering on any specification at remarkable prices for one off pieces; or, once a thing had been developed, to be able to ramp up to very efficient production based on the exact likely demand for the product. Like a quantum version of the Simplex Algorithm, this meant that markets could be fulfilled with maximum efficiency, almost before the market itself existed, and an ongoing recycling pathway which meant the promise of almost zero wastage. It fed the dream of limitless development with almost 100% base energy recycling. A concept which in many ways provided the almost religious zeal that drove the remarkable development of this golden age. And, as the site of Onabule's University and the heart of his scientific and socio-political declarations, it was inevitable that it would be, along with Lagos, his birthplace, a place of pilgrimage and an almost 'religious' centre for the increasing number of people who understood and shared his vision for the world.

Of course, as the 'physical' home of the Global Board and Executive, it also attracted many great administrators who worked within the mechanisms of government. But given the new structure of governance that Onabule had designed, the concept of a 'Capital City' was far more disparate, and the traditions of 'politics' dispensed with, but as a philosophical centre, it was unparalleled and as such attracted many of the world's greatest minds.

Admiral Shadow really did not know what he was looking for, he just knew he needed to find a very special gift and that this was the most likely place on the planet that could fulfil that brief. He stood at a crossroads, rain sliding off his coat leaving no trace on the frictionless material; and looked in all directions. Shadow loved the old and wanted something ageless, and beautiful, but that would still have a use, and most importantly would last a very, very long time. He peered through the rain down the narrowest of the four streets, when suddenly there was a momentary break in the cloud and blistering sunshine came through like laser beam, falling just in front of a tiny shop with lovely decorative windows about fifty meters further along. Admiral Shadow shrugged and headed for the shop, tucking himself into the side of the lane as he dodged the other shoppers before arriving at the strange little shop where he slid inside.

The shop was a crazy mish-mash of electronics and antiques of all sorts. Not just electronica, but of what looked like ancient artefacts, mostly from before the start of the GLF and all piled up without any regard for how much they might be worth, or any account of the risk of damage. Paintings, statues and carvings, TV sets... and even a few CD's all mixed in with old robots and drones and other early bits of AI.

He looked around, and at first could see no one until suddenly he realised that sat at a desk at the very back of the shop was a little old man, head down and dozing with a pair of thick round black spectacles just about hanging onto his ears, swaying back and forth with his breathing, like a tiny double swing. On his head sat what looked like an ancient soldiers cap in a very faded blue and a worn brass pin. He was surrounded by junk and his pockets were crammed full of all sorts of antique paraphernalia, including what Shadow could have sworn was a push button pen. He moved closer, incredibly quietly so as to not disturb the old man, and the Admiral's incredibly quiet involved sliding through the air in such a way as to not create any kind of detectable ripples at all. Nevertheless, and most surprisingly to Shadow, the old man awoke…

'Wa? Was at…erm…ah, herm…yes that's me… yes of course' said the old man, somewhat disorientated, and pushing his small round glasses back up his nose.

'Ah yes, here you are, very good…very good… now Sir, just a moment, let me get myself together' he pulled himself up straight with some effort.

The more Shadow looked the more he realised that this person was a truly remarkable age. Most physical infirmities could be treated without too much effort in modern Mexico City, but unless the shop keeper preferred not to, or didn't have the means, the signs of wear and tear on his body was very evident and did not look as if he had any modifications whatsoever. Not least the fact that he only appeared to have three teeth remaining at the front of his mouth. Shadow was not sure he had come to the right place and was about to start making his excuses, when suddenly his eyes alighted on the corner of an album cover he had only seen online in pictures from very rare vinyl record collections… He pointed – 'Can I have a look at that please' he said, barely able to contain his excitement.

The old man shuffled over and pulled out the ancient record sleeve, which once extracted from the junk around it, looked in remarkably good condition.

'Ah yes' said the old man 'A Love Supreme by John Coltrane – a classic…like your jazz do you?' he said turning to the Admiral, who was feeling a bit deflated, assuming the old man didn't have a clue what the recording was, and hence how much it was likely worth.

'A first edition pressing if I'm not mistaken' said the little old man, depressing Shadow still further. 'Great music for the soul – yes, indeed, now that man WAS a genius' said the old man spinning it in his hands, before putting it on his desk.

'Now then', he said turning back to Shadow 'What was it you actually came in for, as I very much doubt you just wandered in on the off chance that I would be a purveyor of extremely rare, and brilliant, 20th Century jazz recordings, even if that may or may not be the case.'

Shadow now realised that the old man's eyes were piercing, despite the fact that every other part of him appeared decrepit, and that he was clearly no fool.

'I am looking for a gift, something really special that will last a very, very long time, so it needs to be very strong – almost indestructible and something that is unique to..well...the Earth actually. I am just browsing for ideas, but I like 20th Century memorabilia, as you can tell from my...er...taste in music, so I was thinking perhaps some classic old tech, maybe something really distinct'.

The old man's smile slowly spread across his face as he nodded in time to Shadow's words, almost as if he already known what he was going to say and was impatient to wait for him to finish talking.

'Yes, yes, of course I have got exactly the thing you need, it's just the ticket and, not only almost indestructible, but extremely rare – in fact one of a kind, and I know that, because I developed it – many, many years ago of course – not in this rinky dink shop, oh no, no, no – back when I was an engineer of some repute myself you know.. – now then, where is it' he said turning around reaching down and opening a single concealed draw, set just above the floor, and clearly knowing exactly where the mystery item was. He pulled out a black box, embossed around the edges with a fine line of gold, about the size of a small box of cereal. On the front was a faint outline, also in black, of what looked like an old Century digital tablet, and very faintly embossed in the finest gold print, were the words..

BOOK OF BOB

'Hhhmmm…' said the Admiral, not really quite sure what he was looking at.

'Open it' said the old man very quietly.

The Admiral lay it down on the desk before gently applying force on each side of the box to lift the lid away, the suction of the seal initially holding the bottom in place, before with a quiet hiss it slid away, revealing a wrapping of ancient fabric, which Shadow correctly guessed was real silk, folded in an exquisite pattern and hiding the actual object beneath. He carefully unfolded it to reveal an incredibly smooth, dark black and almost entirely featureless tablet. He gently lifted it out of the box, and while it was only thin at little more than five millimetres thick, it was heavier than he expected. He turned it over in his hands, and in certain light he could just about see fine lines of gold running through it, what appeared to be just under the surface.

The most striking thing, however, was the feel of it – for all the world it felt like stone, maybe some kind of highly polished obsidian, a glass forged in the depths of the hottest volcanoes and allowed to cool incredibly slowly.

'Is it actually, just a polished stone?' asked the Admiral, in all seriousness.

The old man cackled 'Well I suppose so, the material is a stone like material, enriched with a Titanium and Tungsten' the circuitry is a gold alloy and the screen is a wafer of carbon lattice – basically a very thin sheet of engineered diamond. This will most likely still be here well after the solar system is just a cinder… If you want something that will last a very long time, there is probably nothing more likely to last than this'.

'So what does it do – I can't see any way of turning it on' said the Admiral spinning it around in his hands.

'Well now' said the old man, as the registered keeper, only I can operate it, but I can gift it to you if you decide to take it'. He held out his hands and Shadow passed the object back to him.

'Now then Bob' said the old man 'how are we feeling today?' Instantly the tablet came alive with lines of gold pulsing beneath the surface and the outline of a screen suddenly glowing with a deep natural light, not a normal synthetic light but almost like the glow of sunrise, and from beneath the diamond screen emerged a Home Screen and an operating system like nothing the Admiral had ever seen before.

The old man launched into what it took Shadow a few moments to realise, a prepared sales pitch... he almost laughed.

'The Book of Bob was designed to be the ultimate tablet and a reference back to the very early days of 'smart' digital tech. It is designed not to require charging, but absorbs power directly from it's surroundings, through the natural properties of the presence of Selenium in it's casing, into it's hugely efficient polonium enriched battery (not serviceable at home)' the last bit said at half volume into his cupped hand.

'The Book of Bob, is pre-programmed with all of human knowledge, art, music and literature as published to date and operates completely independently of any network or cloud service, and as such all this data is permanently embedded into it's almost infinite memory capacity'.

Shadow raised his eyebrows – the use of internal memory had disappeared aeons ago, almost everything operated through cloud services, even within the military the standard was to create distributed resilient data clouds amongst any remote deployed corps, rather than fully independent systems.

'The Book of Bob' the old man continued 'is the perfect gift for anyone who intends to be off grid for very very long periods of time, will be travelling through hazardous and unknown territories, but still requires access to all the great works of man – truly a gift for the modern explorer!'

The old man stopped with a flourish and the Admiral tried not to laugh.

'Very good' he said – can it play me Giant Steps by John Coltrane?' Immediately the tablet came to life and the Admiral could see on the screen some remarkable old footage of several people walking out onto a stage, the unmistakable gait of Coltrane leading the rest, saxophone gripped at the bottom of his swinging and fully extended arm, in what looked like a mid twentieth century jazz club, but incredibly vivid and clear. He was pretty sure he had seen every available video and heard every recording of this track, but he didn't recognise this one. The look and sound of the tablet was truly amazing, almost like looking through a piece of glass into the room itself – He was genuinely astounded.

'Amazing, if I can afford it I will have it'

A little while later he walked out of the shop, two parcels under his arm, the rain had stopped and the hot sun was starting to break through. The old man had thrown in the vinyl and the gift was exactly his budget. The Admiral felt the warm glow of having ticked off a serious item on his to do list. Now he just needed to focus on his mission to Jupiter – he looked up into the sky and could see the test pulses of the huge and awesomely powerful laser at the focus of the power array orbiting the sun, and wondered what the next few years would bring.

Chapter 14 : When the Lights are Low

Shadow stepped past Danny and into the room and was immediately hit by a feeling of nostalgia, as if walking into a sci-fi movie set in the early ages of space travel; a control centre for some of the first missions when only nations could send people into space. He looked around, the lights casting a dark orange with banks of monitors placed between large heavy red structural steel supports set into the wall with ancient keyboards beneath them and a variety of coloured cables running across the floor from one side of the room to the other.

'Let me turn up the lights' said Danny quietly.

He walked over to the corner just opposite the doors and wound a circular knob which steadily brought the lights up to a more acceptable level, moving from orange into a warm yellow glow. Shadow followed his every move, not blinking or taking his eyes off him for even a moment. Full defence protocols had kicked in, automatically driven by his genetic modifications, and every move Danny made was being analysed, his centre of balance and all possible options that Danny may consider if attempting anything foolish.

'So, Danny, what on Earth is going on here?' he said, once the light was up to a more reasonable level. There was no indication that Danny intended trying anything physical, in fact he could see he was being purposefully open and clear in his movements, so it was highly unlikely that he would be able to turn anything around and get the jump on Shadow.

'Well, Mr Shadow, it's a very long story' he said 'in fact it is pretty much the longest story possible, given that it goes back to the very beginning of time...in fact to the event that triggered the Inflation of the Cosmos and, what is generally called the Big Bang, although it wasn't big and it didn't bang, but there you go, the first cosmic joke.'

Shadow, frowned 'What are you talking about exactly' he said, his tone suggesting that he was already beginning to lose patience.

Dan pulled himself up

'OK, please let me introduce myself, and while you will undoubtedly not believe anything you hear at first, you will come to realise that everything I tell you is true.. For I am a Dan, from the eternal line of Dan's, avatar of Bob, the Boltzmann Brain at the beginning and end of all things' said Dan in a grand voice, puffing out his chest...

'You are the what, what, what of what?' said Shadow, suddenly overcome with the desire to laugh... 'Come again Danny, for freaks sake, this sounds priceless but before you do, what on Earth is this room we are stood in exactly?'

Dan turned around and strode over to a light switch beside a large ornate picture frame on the wall, Shadow still following his every move. He flicked the switch and inside the ancient frame a picture from aeons ago appeared.

'It's VE Day, from the World War Two, if you remember that from your history lessons" said Danny

Shadow walked over and looked at the ancient picture. It was a room full of natural people, many dressed in military uniform, men and women smiling and laughing and many looking towards the camera. He recognised the place straight away - it was his club, the Jazz Haus, it had the same arches on the wall, but more than that, he could feel it was the same place; had the same magic ambience, even if the actual footprint of the space was a bit different. Most remarkably, however, was the band suspended on the wall, up above the drinker's heads. A crazy drum kit behind a guy with an accordion perched on the edge of his seat straight in front, ready to go. The picture was so alive he could feel the moment, sense the buzz and chat of conversation in the air, the music, the beer, the morning sunshine streaming through the window. Shadow's eyes scanned across the photo, and suddenly stopped, froze, for there, sat in the middle of the crowd and looking straight into the camera and gently smiling, was Danny...

'Shadow pointed - 'Is that you??' He exclaimed , the photo had to be from almost ten thousand years ago, and no natural human could ever live that long.

'Yes...well kind of - we don't exist as a continuous collection of matter, we more ...emerge..at points through history - generally born in a normal way, in more recent years engineered, chosen at 'random' from a gene pool to create a template from which a mod might be developed, but yes we are born with continuous memories carried forward, or across, from all previous versions.'

'And you said you are 'avatars' of someone or something else - Bob?'' enquired Shadow.

'Yes, that's correct, of Bob, the Boltzmann Brain at the start and end of all things, but we are still made from normal organic matter, so we still think like organic beings, we just have a… higher…more strategic, perspective'

'But, even so' continued Danny 'to communicate across the entire four dimensional space-time structure of the entire universe, we need to be able to transmit from the future to the past as well as carrying memories forward - hence the network of tachyon transmitter stations, such as this one, and the 'stone' tablets as carried by the Dans as we complete our missions.'

'Sorry'' said Shadow 'This is a what?'

'This entire building is a Tachyon transmitter linked to a number of objects called 'the stone tablets', which we have developed over the aeons, made to Bob's design and distributed across the entirety of space and time. They are designed to maintain contact between the Dan's as we fulfil our mission to nudge life into various stages of advancement. We use music, mainly improvised or jazz music, to 'configure' the planetary nodes. In addition the kind of advanced life capable of providing the subjective 'trigger' observations that collapse probability wave functions into actual particles and events, have to be able to appreciate complex music - it's just one of those universal laws that Bob consistently found to be true. I have been broadcasting your last few concerts across the universe which has been, or will be, used by the Dan's to align co-ordinates across the entire expanding and contracting phases of space time;

while also triggering inspiration and enlightenment' events within targeted individuals , who can then lead others along a path to full intellectual 'completion. Therefore creating the kind of stable societies and global ecological systems the Universe needs to keep it 'real', rather than an infinite cloud of 'virtual' quantum probability waves.'

Shadow continued to look dumbfounded...he of course understood the basic quantum mechanics, which high school graduate didn't, but it was not often it was crammed alongside this kind of old-school religious chat.   But the photo looked real, the room was real and pretty crazy and nothing about Danny's body language suggested he was lying...

'It's like a bio-quantum test tone' continued Danny 'A species can only progress and be worthy of continued effort, if they can appreciate and understand complex improvised music. If their minds can make the almost instantaneous intuitive leaps while still keeping track of the structure of the progressing harmony, the interconnectedness of the performers entangled consciousness and the ability for that to communicate to an audience. Basically if a species can do that, then they make reality, but if they can't then they are a dead duck in terms of collapsing quantum events. As such, they are not really much use to us or the rest of the universe, in which case we generally let natural evolution take its course, which almost always, in fact always, leads to extinction within a few hundred years of post-industrial development, if they can even make it that far.'

Danny looked up at Shadow, with a renewed focus in his eyes

'Human kind and it's ongoing evolution through genetic modifications has been a very long standing project of ours. From the arrival of the first Dan when he brought his 'stone tablets', and played to Moses a selection of very nice entry level smooth Jazz, from the species Angeliconians, who then began spreading the teachings inspired by the music he had heard on top of Mount Sinai. Describing it as 'the music of angels' and the enlightened philosophy of fairness and hope as embodied in the Ten Commandments.'

'Are you talking about the pre-Great Leap Enlightenment religions?' Asked Shadow 'All the crazy fairy stories that on more than one occasion almost wiped out human kind due to ridiculous religious wars?'

'Yes, we tried to make the commandments as clear and simple as possible, a very basic framework for people to understand to allow for steady peaceful progress and empathic intellectual development, but at the time huge divergencies kept on appearing between groups of individuals, and bizarrely, very often, the groups who espoused the strongest allegiance to any particular religion appeared to have the most trouble understanding the intention of the commandments - it was a fascinating time to be a Dan'

'Hhmm' said Shadow 'And what about Bob, who the frack is he again..?'

'So Bob is the Quantum Boltzmann Brain which exists at the very beginning and end of the Universe. At the very last 'moment' as a Universe collapses back in on itself, and before Inflation is triggered, the entire matter energy potential of the Universe hangs in a perfectly balanced sphere of entangled quarks (it actually doesn't collapse to a single point, but reaches an equilibrium prior to that) and as such behaves like a single, enormous, quantum computer capable of calculating all possible eventualities of all possible pathways back into an expanding phase once again.'

Danny paused for a moment, before continuing.

'It instantaneously calculates all the probability waves for every particle and potential particle in the Universe, from the beginning to the end of time and back to another collapsing phase through which it basically folds itself back into the box, to create the best possible version of itself. We, the Dan's, are avatars of the brain, nudging things where they can't be made to emerge without us. As far as we can tell, we are an innovation which came out of a number of Bob's early and rather dismal attempts to create a Universe, and we have been around ever since. We are of course, not the brain, but we have the knowledge and are born knowing the mission - we all also completely understand Onabule's set of equations as they set out the best 'in game' version of the forces and parameters that Bob baked into this Universe at the outset. We are here to help keep the whole thing stable, and we are, if I do say so for all of us, pretty good at it...' Dan, raised his eyebrows and smiled once again.

Shadow engaged the mental tools he had been trained to apply to extreme or inexplicable situations, and given the lack of evidence at this point to the contrary, and any other reasonable explanations for what he was seeing, he decided that on the balance of probabilities it might be possible that Danny was telling the truth, and until anything came up that contradicted his explanation, that he might as well just accept it.

'So, just to be clear' said Shadow 'You are broadcasting our gigs across the entirety of space-time and my club is a pan-dimensional faster than light speed jazz radio station?'

'Yes' said Dan 'that's correct'.

'Royalties?' enquired Shadow, with a slight shrug.

Chapter 15 : The Greatest Mind

(2900 AD)

Onabule strode up to the podium – this was actually going to be easier than he thought. After listening to the garbled nonsense that had just come out of the Presidents mouth it would be almost impossible not to rip it all to pieces. Really, he must have been given a briefing document, which would undoubtedly have been written in the most simplistic terms, but he really can't have read it. Clearly he had taken the time to have his hair done and a new 'super-white' shine put on his teeth, but his grasp of even the most rudimentary elements of the long standing aspects of basic physics was woefully short, never mind the cutting edge elements of his new theory.

Ever since Onabule had published his completed theory and equations, his star had risen and risen, as the small pool of physicists and mathematicians began to really test and unravel the meaning within the equations, and slowly the word had spread that every element of it was a complete description of the world of sub-atomic particles while beautifully bridging the apparent inconsistencies with the large scale effects of relativity and the granular nature of Space-Time. The theory was completely consistent with observations, explained why galaxies still managed to cling together despite spinning too fast, explained what and where dark matter was and why it was so undetectable and what was driving dark energy, and predicted it's eventual demise as it ebbed away as the Universe aged and a new phase of contracting space time in the unimaginably distant future.

It completed Einstein's work, describing the physics at play within the various zones of his four dimensional block Universe; describing the forces and particles present within the 'future' and 'past' and the fiendishly complex transitional physics of the 'Now Wave' – the ongoing shockwave generated by Inflation and the Big Bang that condensed the 'probabilities' of quantum waves into the massive and rigid structures which exist in the past. It explained the classic 'double slit' experiment and entanglement, how the equivalent of electromagnetic waves propagated ahead of the Now Wave, almost but not quite entirely in reverse, creating pilot waves that influenced and directed the behaviour of particles as we observed them. And finally, it provided the asymmetry required to explain why matter was so much more predominant than anti-matter in the region of physical space-time that life emerged.

He had finally climbed onto the shoulders of the giants of the 20th Century – the first person in almost a thousand years to do so in any meaningful way – and as such he was now world famous, a truly iconic figure, and he intended to use it to avert the repetition of the failings of the last thousand years.

He had reached the podium and looked out to see Daniella sat in the third row back. He smiled at her as she was already beaming – she knew exactly what was coming next and looked visibly excited; almost on the edge of her seat. After watching so many presentations by politicians standing in front of experts – whether scientists, engineers, business leaders, doctors or almost any group of people who actually knew anything – and talking such extreme garbage while those same experts stood cringing in silence – it was essential that this be done now, while his position as 'the smartest human who ever lived' was pretty much unassailable.

He stepped forward and leaned into the microphone, gripped the sides and took a deep breath before delivering his speech.

'No Mr President, your interpretation of my theory is, I'm afraid, woefully inaccurate in almost every way. In fact I would go so far as to say that your understanding of even the most basic elements of the theory, the ideas derivative of previous, long-standing and established theories as taught in high school, is deeply and profoundly shallow. For me this represents a seriously disturbing trend back to the political landscape of the 21st Century, a time when rhetoric and charisma overshadowed talent, intelligence and ability. A time when the obsession with the nation state stoked up nationalistic divisions between normal people, where politicians manipulated media and regularly misled the public.

This was a time religion was used to promote wars and fanaticism and intellectual fascism.

This was a time when sub-intellect world leaders were allowed to wreak destruction, havoc, mayhem and murder unchecked without any logical restraints in place.

This was a time when sub-intellect world leaders refused to accept that a model of permanent economic expansion within a constrained space could never be sustainable, and ultimately drove the human society to the point of collapse; and the human race to a thousand years of decline as the strategy inevitably led to energy starvation, economic instability and waves of population collapse.

The idea that the worlds resources could be endlessly exploited, even after the evidence was no longer hidden within the papers of a small number of educated scientists, but was impacting on the world for everyone to see – rising oceans, increasing levels of measurable carbon dioxide, decreasing bio-diversity, increasing year on year extreme atmospheric energy events, rising global temperatures! And yet, somehow, the charismatic ignorant were still allowed to rise to the top through the role of dysfunctional democracies which systematically undereducated their own populations, and allowed for leadership to be driven by ignorance rather than expertise and experience. A time when an un-holistic approach to our place within the global eco-system led to rampant pandemics, huge amounts of suffering and death. A time when sociopathic narcissists became the leaders to promote that ignorance, to encourage and embolden stupidity and embed it into education systems. A time when humanity was divided, dislocated and self destructive and a time we must never return to.

What we should have learned from our own history is that the greatest threat to mankind is not an asteroid from space, not a super-eruption nor an solar flare, but incredibly dangerous small conglomeration of matter into a stupid human being, who, despite all the evidence to the contrary, believe they can run a thing as complicated as a civilisation. That despite being repeatedly proven wrong, still believe that we can all benefit from the words that come out of their mouth.

Mr President, I strongly believe your brand of politics… this charming charismatic ignorance, truly threatens the future of human kind and represents a move back to that truly tragic era of human history. We are at such a fragile moment as we claw our way back to stability. We must ensure that our renewed global governmental systems can thrive and plan an unfettered path into the future. We must be able to plan strategies and projects that span, not just years or decades, but entire centuries and millennia. We can't return to the political models of the past, where the least fit person to pilot 'Starship Earth' can be allowed anywhere near the controls – we must move on and create the systems of government that can truly operate on these scales.'

Onabule took a deep breath and pulled himself up to full height, his deep black skin glistening ever so slightly in the heat.

'That is why I today announce that I will be standing in the next election as a Presidential candidate. Not because I think I have all the answers, but because I know that I don't. I believe it is time for us to reform politics in it's entirety and remove power from the politicians and put it into the hands of appointed professionals. My government will work on a complete restructuring of the global parliament, so that the elected politicians act as a non executive board, hiring and firing the very best minds to work on the next phase of the collective human endeavour, but carrying little power beyond that function for themselves. Those that want power can't be allowed to wield it – it must

be given by appointment and controlled by those whose intent is only for the benefit of all people. The elected must have the qualities of only being able to see the best in others. The appointed need to be the best, be paid accordingly and judged only on the results they achieve.

My new theories of physics will unlock untold opportunities – for engineering, for space travel, for biology and managing the planets few remaining resources, for harvesting the energy we need to survive and thrive for the next epoch. We can't afford to leave this in the hands of narcissistic amateurs who think the rest of us can't get enough of hearing what they have to say; when those of us who know, know that what they say makes no sense and that this in some way doesn't matter to everyone else. That we, who have taken the time to become experts and professionals, should stand at the back of these stages' Onabule gestured to the *assemblage of remarkable minds lined up at the back of the platform 'saying nothing but wringing our hands as the intellectual garbage leaves the mouths of those we are supposed to be answering to. There is a bright future for mankind, my equations unlock that future in a way that will only be realisable over the next decades as other great minds work out how to apply this new physics and take us to the places that we have only been able to imagine until now. Thankyou.'*

Onabule put his palms together, nodded his head in thanks and strode from the stage as the President, still half smiling and trying to digest what had just been said, was led away by his aides.

Chapter 16 – One Good Turn

Captain Radisson arrived at his chair in the midst of the bridge just moments before the alarm began to sound, within a fraction of a second his emergency protocols kicked in, his metabolic rate began to rise, controlled by the bio-circuitry embedded throughout his nervous system, and heart rate increased. The screen in front of him was already detailing the conditions that had caused the ships computer to initiate the emergency systems and was starting to consider and present options.

The Captain already knew the problem of course. It was why he had left his quarters hours ago and was in position and ready to respond. In fact, if he had waited for the alarm he would not have had the time to travel the 150 metre's even if sprinting at normal speed, and make the necessary choice, or in fact any choice. The ship was now travelling just over 15000km per second, relative to the Sun, and at that speed any collision would be catastrophic, and so the ship was equipped with a full range of the most sensitive long range scanners ever devised. Not just scanning the electromagnetic spectrum (light / heat / radio waves) the ship was also equipped with incredibly sensitive scanners looking for gravitational wave anomalies and even distortions in the Higgs field. It was these systems that had triggered the alarm and that was currently downloading vast amounts of data to the Captain's screen while simultaneously the ships onboard quantum computer was considering the likely cause of the anomaly and available options to avoid any potential risk.

The Captain could see that as the information came in from the sensors and the computer began building the profile of the object or field that had been detected, that the available options were becoming increasingly limited on the adjacent navigational screen. Of course, he knew all this already and he was desperate to initiate the course adjustments that would be required to arrive at the inevitable outcome, but he had to wait for those very short moments (in fact, the whole process of analysis and option detailing by the ships computer took less than three seconds) before he made his choice and directed the ship to take the only evasive action he was ever going to choose.

The ship made the positive identification, pretty much the worst possible scenario ever considered by the mission planners; a free dark primordial black hole travelling in almost exactly the opposite direction to the ship at a pretty impressive speed itself of almost 300,000kph. While the circumference of the hole was relatively small, less than that of a small moon, it's incredible mass of over two times that of the sun, was creating huge distortions in space time, and even with immediate action, these would not be avoidable by the ship. The ships computer took less than 2 seconds to re-evaluate all options available and the relative impact across the entire mission of each of those options, including the extended mission timescale, alternative mission destinations and ancillary resource implications, such as the need to relocate **HSS1** and re-align the various accelerator lasers and utilisation of other gravitational fields surrounding all stars in the stellar neighbourhood in the line of site of the ship. In fact, it wasn't the calculations that took the time – as a true quantum computer, the ship did it all simultaneously – it was the converting the solutions back into standard language which could be presented on a screen. That extra time would have proved fatal had the Captain not been there and ready to execute his decision. As soon as the options presented themselves, he made the choice, re-aligned the ship as much as was possible, still entering the blackholes outer gravitational field, but ultimately changing the direction of the ship away from Alpha Centauri and the waiting HSS_1. He understood the implications and could imagine the crews likely reaction, but from the available options it was as good as any other, but more importantly it aligned perfectly with his own agenda.

'Eridani?!' Said Lioux, Chief Navigator 'We are now going to Eridani..!?' she said again 'that is going to add some serious miles onto the cruise'.

The cruise was how the crew referred to their 250 year voyage through deep space. 'Well, actually it is 82G Eridani, first of all at least, but basically, yes that's right – not many choices to be honest and at least that allows us to keep on building speed before we sling shot around the star, look at the exo-planets we already know are there, maintain a decent amount of our velocity.'

'So how long is that going to add to the voyage..?'

'Well, we still have several choices to make along the way, and depends on how we keep on increasing our own speed or not, what that does to our ability to turn without losing too much velocity, the actual path, whether we go via Sirius and use the huge mass of that star for the final turn back towards the Earth but all in all, for us, without taking into account our ability to run slow, so actual ship time…er… about 1250 years… So' said Radisson, rolling his eyes as if calculating in his head the huge number of variable parameters, 'depending on how close we get to light speed, which is pretty close now the engine is fully operational, and given the time dilation effects as described by Special Relativity' he paused 'about 8200 Earth years…'

There was a stunned silence in the room.

'So that is gunning it and a great huge loop around the Southern sky basically' said Lioux quietly…

'Yes, we will travel over 200 light years, even though our furthest distance from the Sun will be less than 30 Light Years, it's just how to maintain the velocity...'

He understood the crew's horror, even for them, their ability to run incredibly slowly and with staggeringly long expected lifespans, the prospect of spending so much time inside the HSS2 felt daunting and intensely claustrophobic. He knew that they would have some respite, but at the moment he could not reveal the full extent of the plan.

'The next step is to send a signal back to Earth, let them know what has happened and build up a new mission plan – that's all going to take some time, so lets focus on what we have to do, get all necessary intel and prepare for the immediate matter to hand; the pass around the black hole and make sure we survive that, and get as much amazing science done from that opportunity in the process.'

The crew looked around at each other, with the level of expertise and training on board, there was a realisation that this was going to be the most remarkable opportunity in the history of human exploratory science, and they could see the sense in the Captain's words; they had to make the most of it. For the next ninety days at least, as the black hole came closer as they moved along the new flight plan, they would be able to see into the heart of the galaxies most exotic stellar object for the first time in human history and interrogate it with the ships remarkably sensitive probes. After that would be several hundred years to catch up on a bit of sleep...

Chapter 17: Hello from TRJS Jazz!

The band stood and sat around the stage with Danny perched on the edge of Kato's amp.

'So, what you are saying is, music, most specifically improvised music such as jazz, is incredibly important for the development of intelligent species across the Galaxy…'

'Universe' Danny interrupted, (not something that Georgia was used to…)

She took a deep breath…'And that we are broadcasting. via this building, which is in fact a Tachyonic Radio Jazz Station, to the entire Galaxy..'

'Well, more the local neighbourhood of stars at the moment' Danny corrected again 'but yes, essentially that is correct'

'And you started building this place over ten thousand years ago'.

'Well, not me exactly, emergent forms of me, or me of them – mostly real people, not just genetically identical to me but with actual identical molecular brain structure and with shared memories – all of which formed apparently at random. We, the Dans' are placed at very specific points in space time to nudge events in just the right way, largely to promote the ongoing development of intelligent species across the Universe. As you probably know, a requirement for a stable Universe is intelligent life, as they…you… collapse the wave function into actual particles and events.   A measure of the required level of intelligence is the development of music, and specifically in higher forms, the ability to intuitively create music instantaneously, which on Earth, is the music you know of as jazz'.

'So why don't you just make the jazz and keep it all ticking along' Said Red frowning.

'I can't' replied Danny

'Why not?'

'Tone deaf...no talent...what can I say, I just don't have the music in me...never have had... just not part of Bob's plan'.

'And Bob is...'

'The Boltzmann Brain formed in the timeless and infinite quark plasma at the beginning and end of all things – look it up, Bolzmann Brains are actual things – the idea tends to pre-date Onabule, but it is a real idea – a mind that most likely forms in infinities' said Shadow, who had already looked it up.

'So, talking of Onabule' said Kato quietly 'He made it clear nothing could travel back in time, that everything behind the Now Wave was frozen and nothing could be changed. So what are these signals we are sending if not changing things'.

'Aahh well' said Danny 'I am of course, very glad you asked me that, because that is very much the crux of the matter and at the heart of this particular situation'. He pulled himself up 'The thing is, that, well I am quite sorry to say, that, well…non of you actually exist yet, at least not within the frame of the Now Wave, and most likely never will – you see, this is the Future realm of Space Time, where, as I think you know, multiverses are almost infinite, and you inhabit a particularly unlikely branch of this almost infinite multiverse.'

He looked around at the stunned faces...

'Just think, a ten thousand year old jazz club at the end of time, in a musical junk yard, an elite commander abandoning his corps to build the place, just the right thing popping up just as it's needed...all sounds pretty unlikely doesn't it. I mean, look at the Sun – ever wondered why it's so red? It shouldn't be really, but it's light is kind of in between not quite there or not there at all, the energy split across countless dimensions; just like everything else – you are all here and not here...I think you probably know that's true – like ghosts of things that could be'.

'The thing is this' he continued 'this is not just an unlikely possible future, this is right out there on the very edge of what could be. In fact, most Earth futures are pretty dreadful – apocalypses, unstoppable global warming, pandemics which decimate either the entire human race, or entire families of animals or plants, which makes it impossible for the human race to survive'. There is just so many different ways for the human race to destroy itself that finding a future like this one, which kind of settles into a fairly boring monotonous hedonistic stability, and then contains someone who is fanatical about jazz, and a band of musicians still capable of performing it! Well, that was not easy at all – and there has been many versions of me who have come to pretty nasty ends looking!'

Danny looked around at every face in turn, a slightly apologetic half grin on his face.

'Wow – well that is a show stopper' nodded Kato 'So if this isn't now, when is now now?!!'

Captain Daniel Raddison had worked with the crew to develop the final mission plan and send back to Earth. He already knew where they were going of course but they had to go through the process of developing up the plan, realising that they couldn't get the go-ahead from Earth as it would take too long for the signals to travel back and forth, and therefore taking the executive decision to proceed.

While they could use the small reservoir of entangled particles held on board the ship, mirrored by an identical reservoir on Earth, the amount of data that would be transferred would pretty much eat up the entire store, so that provided the perfect excuse not to.

Of course, he could just tell his crew mates who he was really – an avatar of Bob, but there had been many permutations of that continuum tested within the Future Realm, ahead of the Now Wave, and they almost entirely concluded with the Captain being declared mad, arrested and confined to his quarters, so it had to be the slow way.

The crew already knew they would arrive back to a world where they recognised no one, where they would continue to live as generations of people came and went, or that might not even survive at all. So they had quietly acquiesced to the logic of taking the long way home. At least it gave them all time to think and study and learn more than any other human had ever before.

Now that the course was set and the plan agreed, he could initiate his part within the grand scheme, and so here he was, in the dead of night climbing into one of HSS2's four transit pods with a small case of belongings in one hand and the tablet that he had been gifted by the Admiral in the other (The perfect excuse for getting one of Bob's ancient stone tablet devices onboard HSS2 without raising any suspicions, this one being the exact same one shown to Moses on Mount Sinai). He had already bypassed the main ship computer and so there would be no notification of his departure until he had left the ship and was well on his way, at which point a holographic message would be broadcast to the rest of the crew.

The plan for the HSS2 was to maintain speed and take several huge loops around the group of stars which surrounded Earth, following huge distortions in space time produced by each of the stars gravitational fields, rendezvousing with HSS1 at critical points along the way for course direction alterations or to aid in decelerating when entering a star system at a very particular direction and velocity to sling shot out again, which ultimately, and most significantly, would bring the ship very close to the massive star Sirius before curving back towards the Earth.

And as they did so they would study and learn, observing interstellar space and dropping probes around planets and into stellar systems to provide data to be transmitted back to Earth. Many of the original mission planners had actually considered something similar as a far better use of the HSS2 in the first place, but the political benefits of sending a group of astronauts to the closest star, to orbit, explore the planets and then return home within a conceivable time frame, was altogether more appealing, low risk and perceived to be more humane as far as the astronauts themselves were concerned.

However, the problem with not arriving at Alpha Centauri, was the ability to be able to slow down enough to enter into a stellar orbit and then speed back up enough to allow for the Dark Matter Cyclone Engine to kick in and accelerate out again. While the ship could slow down using its own systems, this had to be very slow and involved dumping vast amounts of rotational energy from the spinning neutron shell inside the engine, transferring back into a photon beam and firing it out of the front of the ship against the direction of travel. The science fiction fantasy of just dropping out of 'hyper-speed' into a planetary orbit just wasn't possible as this involved, for a ship the size and mass of the HSS2, dumping so much energy, mainly in terms of heat and light, in a short space of time that it would destroy the ship and incinerate half the planet it was attempting to come into orbit around.

Some theorists had played around with converting the excess energy back into dark matter over a shorter period of deceleration, but the technical challenges of this were thought to be too considerable during the initial stages of the mission planning. Over the entire 500 year mission planning period, no agency successfully demonstrated an engineering solution for this model and so the two ship solution remained the only viable option.

In fact, Captain Radisson, utilising the real world on ship observations and experiments, had already started developing a series of applied calculations and schematics, in which he described how the excess energy could be dumped as dark energy (skipping the dark matter phase), creating a bubble of hyper inflation around the ship, which would allow for a rapid re-acceleration again. His work was far from done, but he tasked a team on board to continue the work and run tests as the voyage progressed. While the process had to take place in a very short space of time, and involved accelerating the engine to its theoretical limit, it made the ship altogether more practical when it came to stopping and starting, or at least slowing down and speeding up. However, for the time being his plan involved the ship spending some time cruising around the Southern Sky and passing back near his location but in the opposite direction, in almost a thousand years time, at which point he hoped that the team would have progressed these new engineering concepts a little more so that they could slow down fairly rapidly as the ship once again entered the solar system and approached the Earth.

Another thing that Captain Raddison did not reveal to any of the crew, was that he was, in fact, going to be one of the 'probes' and that he would be leaving the ship during the series of loops to descend to the surface of the fourth planet in the Eridani system, to deliver a very important message to the rapidly evolving people who were in the very early stages of developing a global civilisation.

The tablet that Admiral Shadow had very kindly brought on board provided the link to the Danny based over eight thousand years in one of the many futures ahead of the Now Wave. He and the music of the tablet would inspire and catalyse the Eridanians brains to be able to think laterally, work intuitively and cohesively and develop higher intellectual instincts to progress to the higher plane of thought that allowed them to look out, observe the universe, and in doing so help make it real. At the same time it would allow the Tachyon transmitter to lock onto his exact position in relative space time and allow the network of Dan's to co-ordinate the various nudges required to align against all their various objectives, for Earth, Eridani and the incredibly small number of other planets across the Galaxy which also harboured the potential for intelligent life.

The Captain settled himself into the modules seat, taking one last look around the cabin to ensure all systems were set as intended. It was going to be quite a ride as the module would take a course very close to Eridani itself, losing speed to the stars gravity and after several highly elliptical orbits, settling into the fourth planets orbital plane before finally settling into a planetary orbit and ultimately a re-entry. The whole process would take a number of Earth years, but for the Captain it would only feel like a few weeks.

Finally, with all systems checked, the Captain undocked the pod, gently moving away from the side of the HSS2 and, with the tiniest of pulses from the small ships thrusters, curved out into the darkness of interstellar space, still moving at an incredible speed, the pod would slowly drop behind the main ship, protecting itself within the field generated by the Dark Matter engine until it would twist away and head directly for the Eridani system.

However, the real challenge for the Captain did not begin until he made planet fall. His mission was to identify and inspire a small number of super-charisma messiah type individuals who would act as the 'butterflies wings' of change, producing tiny ripples which would grow into massive social evolution over many hundreds of years. All the time, working behind the scenes to promote creative and cultural activity, developing and funding music venues, theatres and promoting great artists and supporting their work. Of course, the Captain was not Eridianian, neither genetically nor in looks, as humans were much, much smaller, but as it happened, a strange twist of fate had led to the evolution of a hominid like species who the dominant Eridiani's treated as pets. In fact, they loved them and while they could be fairly brutal with one another, they would pretty much do anything if it made the hominids appear happy. It was Captain Daniel's plan to introduce jazz dance as a particularly expressive way to demonstrate his effusiveness and in doing so start to slowly encourage the art of scat singing amongst his

Eridiani masters, which in time should turn into fully evolved tradition of musical improvisation!

Of course, it was going to be quite difficult pretending to be a dumb animal while cajoling a species much lower on the evolutionary scale to develop jazz, but with a bit of luck it wouldn't be too long before a resident Eridiani 'Dan' emerged and he would have some intellectual stimulating company to enjoy as well as a partner to work with.

In the meantime, he would literally be the organ grinder disguised as the dancing monkey – a very long way from the Captain of a super advanced interstellar star ship…But, as he was in effect immortal, he could see that this would be a very short episode in a very long life. Furthermore, he would be able to see the entire process of social and cultural evolution, stepping in and tuning or nudging ever so slightly as and when required, across the entire span of the cultural evolution of an entire society.

And once completed, he still very much intended re-joining the **HSS2** as it looped back through the Eridani system some one thousand years later heading in the opposite direction. If everything went to plan (and the crew of the **HSS2** followed his precise instructions), the Eridian's burgeoning interplanetary space race would, by that time be up and running with a series of space flights, initially tested by their beloved hominids, of which he very much intended being one of the first test pilots, putting him in the path of the HSS2 and a ride back to Earth.

A very big plan, with a lot to go wrong, but he did, after all, have the benefit of hindsight, even if that hindsight came from many thousands of alternative possible futures.

The pod swung behind the main ship, hung there for a moment, before sweeping off into the darkness, heading for the light of the still distant star system.

Chapter 18 – On Tour

'So', said Danny, as he casually walked back from the bar carrying a case of drinks to share out (after being mindful to leave the appropriate holo credits floating above the till), 'The real benefit of this particular continuum is that we are about to witness two of the most remarkable events in human history, and for the occasion, we definitely need a beer'. He started passing out the bottles 'in addition' he said as he casually flipped the bottle tops from the bottles as he passed them out, 'we are definitely in the best possible place for both these particular events'.

Shadow had felt a bit out of his depth for the last few hours, but the possibility of risk and danger were familiar territory for him, and so he suddenly started to feel a bit more at ease.

'And what are those' he asked quietly.

'Well the first' said Danny with a big grin 'and it's a good job it takes place in this order...is the return of the HSS$_2$ from it's remarkable interstellar mission around our corner of the Galaxy'

'The HSS$_2$ – the ship sent into space thousands of years ago – was that even real' said Georgia,

'I thought they proved it was a hoax, no such ship ever went anywhere'

'I heard they spent trillions for it to crash into a rock in the Kuiper Belt' said Kato – 'a massive waste of Earth's resources before they gave up on any ideas of interstellar travel'

'It was real' said Shadow 'It's where my saxophone and the Songbook came from – we all know it in our family, the Saxophone was gifted to my ancestor by the Captain of the HSS2 ...know one knew why...it was such an odd gift... And the Captain' he said, spinning back around to Danny 'was called Daniel Raddison! Was that you..???'

'Well' said Danny again, clearly enjoying himself 'you are definitely catching on and yes, the Captain of the starship, was, and still is, one of the versions of me and I still remember the meeting as if it was me – your ancestor was most definitely surprised, but I would say pleasantly so – he loved jazz, discovered it all by himself and was a huge fan'.

'Anyway, let's put the holo-news on and see what we see, and if I am right and the ship has arrived in the solar system, you can all start believing me?!' he said holding his beer in the air.

They turned on the news and instantly the screen showed the image of a remarkable and very large space craft being escorted by a number of smaller craft. The HSS_2 was passing by Mars which was visible behind the image of the ship and clearly filmed from another craft as the starship roared passed. The narrator was jabbering at high speed, but there was no doubt that this was the ship that had left the

Earth's orbit over eight thousand years earlier and this was an Earth shattering event, especially as most people in 12020 did not believe the ship had ever really existed.

'Well then, that looks real enough' said Shadow over the top of his beer and peering out of the window and up into the night sky as if the thing was going to sweep into view over the piles of twisted metal which surrounded the club. 'So what's the other amazing thing that is about to happen'

'Well then' said Danny 'significantly more disturbing…that would be the arrival of the black hole which deflected the HSS2 in the first place' he looked around the room, still grinning but looking slightly less cocky than before…

'How come we never heard of no black hole' grunted Kato 'I am sure that we would have…

of course, they would never have told us that would they...

'Well' said Danny 'The thing is this, the black hole itself is not going to collide with us, but it will eat up a big chunk of the Kuiper belt, and most likely Uranus and Neptune, but the Earth, Mars Saturn and Venus; and the Sun, are most likely going to get pulled into a very tight orbit around it, pretty close but not going over the event horizon, and be carried off towards the inner Milky Way in something of a General Relativity time bubble. As you know the strong gravity field will slow down light, and therefore time itself, and so the Earth will be around for most of the entire history of the Universe' Danny informed the room, even though everybody in the room very much understood elementary level Gen Rel and didn't need it explaining 'Pretty cool in itself, but we, my friends have a whole different path opening up before us'.

'Oh indeed' said Red, feeling more than slightly irritated by Danny's patronising, theatrical manner.

'Oh yes' said Danny 'for we, my friends, are going on tour, taking in the sights, sounds and civilisations of this outer spiral arm, bringing the sound of jazz to this galactic region, and that' he said gesturing towards the TV screen and the HSS2 'is our tour bus!'

Georgia suddenly started to giggle 'Are you for real – you know baby, I am digging your scene but honestly if you are shitting us, I am going to absolutely break your b...'

Suddenly Shadow stepped forward 'OK Danny, what's the plan, and by that I mean first, evidence of black hole story and secondly, if all that is true, how are we going to get into orbit and then onto the HSS_2 given the speed it's likely travelling and the fact that we have no ship'. How long have we got and how do we get to where we need to be?'

The idea of an interstellar tour was definitely rocking Shadow's boat, even if it meant leaving his beloved club.

'Well if you would like pick up your instruments and follow me' said Danny 'Leave the bigger stuff, I have a full range of drum kits and keyboards already packed on your shuttle and, please lets be quick as, while the HSS_2 is only just passing Mars, it is still going at quite a pace, decelerating hard and is going to be here very soon, with the blackhole not all that far behind, and we really do not want to get stuck in it's gravitational field or we will not be going anywhere'.

Everybody wandered out of the door and into the dark night. It was always a bit spooky in the yard when the club was closed and lights off; and tonight there was a strong wind whirling dust devils and litter about the place, howling through the twisted metal of the junkyard and catching on the street lights which hovered just above the perimeter wall. Danny walked ahead, confidently heading straight for a particularly high twisted mound of metallic junk which had no obvious pathway through it.

'I've been working on this for some time' Danny called over the wind to Red and Shadow who were walking just behind and either side of Danny.

'What, the junk yard?' said Red

'Well, actually, that's not what I meant, but yes, it is in fact true'

They reached the edge of the towering pile of rubbish and Danny reached out and pulled on what appeared to be the slide of an old trombone. As he pulled it a retina scan pulsed across his face very briefly, and then a jagged crack appeared in the pile of instruments and slowly began to open.

'Just through here', said Danny, gesturing into the dark hole. They both walked through, closely followed by Kato, Chill and Georgia, all carrying various instruments grabbed from the stage.

They walked down a short dark corridor, lit from the floor with a subdued red light which pulsed very slightly. The corridor opened out into a much larger space, and there in the centre was a ship that was the shape and size of a large transit van with what looked like two small jet engines attached to each side. The shuttle had clearly been built from the junk of the yard. All around the edge was work benches and electronic machinery, much of it old and decrepit, but alongside the vintage stuff was a range of large cutting edge engineering tools and 3D metal printers, along with two large robotic arms sat either side of the shuttle, and some hefty pneumatics and control interfaces. Towards the back of the space was the familiar outline of an old nuclear fusion module, the familiar donut shape half covered in junk and with wires trailing around the workshop, powering the various pieces of equipment, but with two thick cables running to the two engines. Despite the various bits of archaic equipment, it was possibly one of the most advanced engineering labs on the planet, Shadow thought to himself, but the shuttle itself had not been designed with any aesthetic in mind.

'This flies?' said Shadow with a look of total amazement.

'Yep, it's a modified version of one of the old asteroid working shuttles, but I have put a couple of Potter-Onabule engines on either side to give it a bit more...go! said Danny, grinning again. 'They have been charging for over 16 years now, the rotational energy held in the proton shell inside the engines are truly awesome! You can feel it can't you?'

And they could, the air thrummed with the power, space time itself was being twisted into a vortex inside the two closed engines.

'We need to get on board' said Danny 'I can't open up the engines until we are clear of the junk, so we need to get in and get going as they really need to be unleashed or they won't be able to hold the power much longer'.

Danny went to the side of the ship, touched a panel and doorway started to drop, hinged at the bottom, and light streamed out of the ship and into the incredible workshop void under the junk. They all climbed aboard and rapidly orientated themselves inside the ship. Red was instantly familiar with the control surfaces and interfaces, it really was basically like one of the old mining ships she had used when she worked in the asteroid belt. Behind the pilot and co-pilots seats were individual integrated transit suits – each one clearly designed for each of the guys to sit in like a high tech human shaped sarcophagus. Once they were in place, the suits would completely enclose them to protect against the enormous G forces they would experience. Shadow, Red and Chill had used them before, but for Kato and Georgia they were a completely new experience.

'What're these?' asked Georgia rather suspiciously

'Transit suits' said Red 'Believe me, you will be grateful to have them'

'And what's through there', said Georgia again, gesturing at the door to the rear of the cabin'

'The instruments or course!' laughed Danny 'Please take your seats, this baby is ready to go!'

Everyone jumped into their individual seats and the suits immediately began to close around each of them. They could hear the sound of creaking metal as the junk pile opened itself up to reveal the remarkable ship hidden within, before all sound was cut off and the inside of the suit was momentarily completely silent before all the various suit sensors, cameras and microphones kicked in and multiple views of the inside and outside of the ship appeared on the eye screens within the suits.

'OK, this is it' yelled Danny just as the door closed and sealed and through the front windscreen they could see the cloudy sky above. He hit a green button on the control surface, and the entire ship began to throb with power before suddenly leaping into the air and accelerating into the sky at a truly remarkable speed, pressing them all back into their seats.

Chapter 19 – Monkey Man

Captain Radisson sat back into his chair, the huge screen in front of him alight with the magnified view of the Earth, Moon in the foreground, and various other dots of light which were the many space stations which surrounded the planet. Of course, although he would prefer to look out of the window, the final powerful phases of deceleration the ship was applying to bring the ship close into the planet at the speed required to complete this part of his mission, was considerable, so the captain and crew were all seated in reverse position, ship inverted and looking backwards from where they had come as the G-forces pressed them into their seats.

They would cover the distance between Mars and Earth in a little over one week, suffering G's of around 2.5 that of Earth, which even though they were engineered for it, was uncomfortable for such a long period of time.

Of course, time to the crew of the HSS_2 had a totally different meaning to that of most humans, they had already been alive for a little under one thousand five hundred years, the ships actual clock running behind that of the Earth due to the time dilation caused by the different relative velocities (as described in Einsteins equations of Special Relativity), but their own personal clocks screwed far more by the hyper slow metabolic rate they had been designed to operate for most of the time.

Of course, the Captain's was different again from most of the crew, as he had spent almost one thousand years on Eridani 3, hidden amongst the population as a lesser species to the dominant Eridanis. Initially he had acted as a performing monkey and then, as the civilisation developed, a family pet. Throughout his stay on the planet, he had worked his way into a number of influential homes, quietly dropped suggestions, guided decisions and as the technology had developed, hacked into and infiltrated systems to guide the civilisation towards increasing levels of sophistication. However, the Eridani's aesthetic and cultural development remained stunted and Radisson had known that they would never develop into a stable society unless they developed their creativity, especially once he removed himself from the planet; and it was imperative that he kick started the species creative, artistic, cultural and most importantly, musical development before he left, or they would undoubtedly fail as a civilisation.

The Captain smiled to himself, it was the final move in the thousand year plan that was the masterstroke – in one go he appealed to the entire race to develop their creativity while making his final escape. He had placed himself at the heart of the fledgling space programme as a test animal, and as the first creature sent into orbit around Eridani 3, he would be the star of the most watched programme of all time. So, once into orbit, he dispensed with the performing monkey act, explained to an astonished planet who he really was, that they needed to connect with their inner soul through music, and, before igniting the thrusters to push the ship out of orbit and back into the path of the returning HSS_2, he broadcast the live performance by Shadow and the My Funny Quarantine band. The transmission from Dizzy Gil's had been sent back through time by the clubs Tachyon transmitter and picked up by the tablet he had been given by the Admiral before leaving Earth (which he had hidden in the fabric of his seat). As he orbited the planet, he broadcast the entire show to the astonished Eridanis before cruising off into the eternal blackness to the final bars of Somewhere Over The Rainbow.

It still made him laugh, he imagined some of his former owners, and the scientists involved in the space programme, and wondered at the impact such a cultural shock was likely to have.

Of course, they had to go back, take the band and do a show – just to make sure that they had got the message…and to cash in on the acclaim that the band would no doubt receive once they arrived. As the Earth was to head off into the interstellar depths, dragged by the black hole, a new civilisation had to take up the mantle, provide the subjective observations which would collapse the wave functions out of which the Universe was made into real events. Frozen within a super slow region of space time, the Earth was going to have a very different path as it orbited on the very edge of the approaching black holes event horizon, definitely not the place for a hot new band... This time the captain laughed out loud, attracting some curious looks from his crew mates, before he brought himself back under control.

The ship continued to dump energy into the dark energy field it was generating in around itself, inflating a local sphere of rapidly expanding space time, already several thousand kilometres wide, which was now pushing out against the rest of the universe, distorting the distance the ship appeared to be travelling relative to everything else. The path they were taking between the Earth and moon had to be exactly right as they moved through the system before accelerating away again, undoubtedly to the amazement and mystification of the people of Earth.

'Hold on' said Danny to the rest of the band, 'We are crossing over into the HSS2 phase space – it's going to feel a bit weird, a bit like being stretched and squeezed at the same tiiiiimmmmmmeeeennnnn'

To the others, Danny's face appeared to stretch itself across the front of the ship. Not that they noticed as they were also going through a very strange transition into the expanded local bubble of space time which surrounded the HSS_2. The small shuttle was actually moving at some pace, having been running at 2G for several hours and accelerating in the same plane as the HSS2, but heading away from it, aiming to be scooped up by it's deflection field as it passed by. For this to work, they really needed to be matching the massive ships speed as closely as possible and, as the crew were busy trying to adapt to being somewhat larger than they had been moments before, the ship automatically kicked in with a last strong burst of speed, twisting into the HSS2's electromagnetic and gravitational wave field lines before finally and delicately coming to rest in one of the ships docking bays.

As soon as it did so, the Captain Radisson re-engaged thestarship's Potter-Onabule engine, sucked the energy back in from the bubble of expanded space time and gunned the ship back towards the outer solar system and deep space beyond, leaving the entire population of the planet Earth completely mystified until they were swept into the orbit of the black hole following on behind which pretty much froze the planet in a stasis field.

Not that the residents of Earth experienced it in that way, to them life pretty much continued as before, apart from the coming and going of the local universe and visible stars suddenly started to accelerate and slowly disappeared (before eventually reappearing again as the balance of gravity, dark energy and dark matter shifted in favour of a collapsing universe) over the following thousand years or so as each Earth year was equivalent to many thousands of years in the Universe as a whole.

Of course, the story of the arrival and rapid disappearance of the legendary space ship, the HSS$_2$ – the only real attempt by mankind to reach the stars, was passed down through the generations, and eventually returned to mythical status amongst the diminishing population who cruised towards the Big Crunch in the remarkable time bubble that The Earth had become as the last days approached.

Chapter 20 : Goodbye Neptune

Shadow and the band climbed out of the small ship, staggering around the bay, disorientated from the rapid expansion of their local space time, including all the atoms of their own bodies.

Danny shouted at them all to move towards the docking bay door just as a contingent of the HSS_2 crew ran in and pulled them out and along a corridor at speed, before turning into a crew transit area and rapidly strapping the arrivals into another row of almost identical transit suits, which this time they sat down into without much question at all. Once completed, the crew members themselves immediately froze, returning to their natural hyper slow state, just as the ship appeared to tumble over in a very disorientating manner as down became up and then down again as the ship switched from decelerating to re-engaging the engines in line with the direction of travel to re-accelerate again.

To the outside observer, the whole tumbling manoeuvre was a remarkable spectacle as the ships space time contracted, the actual space around the ship being sucked back into the Potter-Onabule engine, the ship itself shrank and then started to disappear, accelerating at a steadily increasing velocity away from the

Earth once again, building up to a steady 1G force.

Over the centuries, the crew had tuned the engine, working with the Captain's schematics and revised calculations, to provide this almost constant thrust which allowed for the ship to reach much higher velocities than had been originally envisioned. They had also been able to adapt the sensors and deflective field in front of the ship to produce enhanced protection, and during the period of their voyage only ever had one close collision with one small piece of interstellar space rock.

Moving at a constant 1G of acceleration would allow the ship to approach light speed in around one Earth year, at which point unmanageable relativistic effects would take hold and time relative to the rest of the Universe would slow to almost nothing. In fact, if the ship kept moving at this relative speed, the space around it would contract and from the perspective of the crew they would be able to cross the entire galaxy in a little under 12 years, however the time dilation effect would mean that in the outside Universe, over 110 thousand years would have passed – not useful when aiming to arrive at your destination within living memory of a particular event, such as an orbital experimental monkey explaining that he was in fact an emissary of a highly advanced civilisation, while also being an Avatar of Bob, a Bolzmann Brain built from a spontaneous Quark Quantum Computer at the beginning and end of all things; and that it was essential that the population of said planet develop the ability to freely improvise music if they were to survive, for reasons which were pretty vague at best, but was, from bitter experience, proven to be true. This was the challenge that Captain

Radisson faced as he accelerated the ship back towards Eridani 3 and the confused and somewhat expectant population of that particular planet.

The Captain swung his seat around as his new guests entered the bridge of his ancient ship, looking around them in bewildered amazement before all locking eyes on the video screen positioned on the wall behind the Captain, and clearly looking back into the solar system and the site of the approaching black hole.

'Hello there' said the captain cheerfully, as the screen displayed the cataclysmic sight of Neptune being ripped apart and sucked across the black holes event horizon, expelling a whole planets worth of energy as it did so. 'Cup of tea?' he looked over his shoulder '…or something a little stronger?'.

Epilogue – A Perfect Night (2019 AD)

Daniel walked out of the wings in the TV studio, he really wasn't comfortable with this amount of public exposure, after millennia of working in the shadows to suddenly have to step into the limelight was really not what he had bargained for. It was a last minute change of plan that had brought him to this point, a new directive coming through from other Daniels, working in the future realm of space time, that had pushed for this radical departure from The Plan.

It was hugely risky, but to have let the red head kid take the lead in what was to be one of the most important film franchises of all time would have been disastrous. Most continuum indicated the films would be scrapped after the second movie in the series as the fans slated the depiction of the lead character in their favourite books as dreadful, having a calamitous effect on the creative and intellectual development of human beings for many hundreds of years, reducing the emerging trend of reading in young people which would have such an impact in future years. Ultimately it would derail the Great Leap Forward as Onabule would not have the work referred to in his Theory of Everything to build upon, the decrepit World Government of politicians would not be replaced by his Council of the Best Minds, which would never be established. So this was essential, he had to step into the limelight, which also meant he had to appear on this show and accept that the risk was worth it.

Not that he minded the host, his natural Irish wit and conversation, and meeting many of the other incredible guests. No, it was the fact that every time he appeared on the show, he brought up the whole Time Travelling thing – that little meme by the band who had spotted his likeness in the photo from the club in Manchester; Band on the Wall, that would many, many years in the future become Dizzy Gill's and the home of the My Funny Quarantine band. An earlier version of himself had been there, fitting out some of the initial mechanical and electrical components of the pan dimensional radio station that the building had actually been designed to be.

He walked into the middle of the set, smiling broadly, waving at the crowd, and glasses in place as the host came over and shook him warmly by the hand and invited him into his seat before inviting on the next guest. He sat back into the expensive red sofa, enjoying the moment, and looking out into the camera lens. Of course, he thought, it will all be fine, no one could possibly know the real reason for him being there and anyway, it was all just part of Bob's big plan.

Eridani 968 AD (After Dan - sometime after 12270 Earth time)

Shadow walked out onto the stage inside the immense arena, a beautiful warm evening with the two moons shining full in the sky, and flocks of gliding insect like creatures catching the updrafts as they floated down from the distant blue mountains, waving out at the cheering crowds of Eridanis, closely followed by the rest of the band, grinning widely, apart from Georgia who remained even more cool than ever. The Eridani's were hugely enthusiastic to welcome the stars from Earth who had inspired the cultural revolution on the planet, ushering in their own golden age of intellectual and social development. Since the departure of Captain Radisson and the bombshell of his transmission from their societies first orbiting satellite, they had worked tirelessly to develop their own technology, culture and, most importantly, music, and as such they had rapidly ushered in their own Great Leap and a period of unimaginable development and peace.

They found it hugely amusing, and humbling, that the species who had guided them to their enlightenment was so similar in appearance to their own beloved pets, and as a mark of love and the compassion they had built them their own small arenas where they could kick footballs to each other, which they were incredibly good at and very much enjoyed.

In the meantime, they had studied jazz, allowed their minds to develop the freedom and intuition to instantaneously improvise music, which became a central part of all Eridanis education within all schools, and music making began to infiltrate every part of their society. Of course, in many ways and after many decades of change, most Eridani's were now more accomplished than the stars of the My Funny Quarantine band stood on the stage, but that did not matter – this was the band who had started it all and for many, this was the only place to be on this truly historic night.

The band walked over to their instruments, and after a moment to check and tune up, kicked into Over the Rain to the roars of appreciation from the whole audience as many started to sing the opening refrain. This was a moment that Shadow had dreamt of and was undoubtedly the greatest moment of his life – he could feel his saxophone come alive in his hands as the notes tumbled out of the instrument completely effortlessly and the whole band locked together perfectly. A perfect moment on a perfect night.

Chapter 21 – And so…

Danny wandered around the workshop a little longer, occasionally looking over at the shuttle he had built over the last few years. The quantum cage scan and transmission would be almost complete, at which point he would have to open the suits, which were in fact mind boggling quantum transition space scanners which, despite the uncertainty principle, could map the complete quantum state of an entire person and broadcast the exact atomic details of the contents to another place in space time via the shared collection of entangled particles which were linked to the set stored on the passing HSS2. Of course, when he opened the suits he was going to have to explain to the band what was really happening – that copies of each of them had been transmitted to the passing HSS2 and that they would not be making the actual journey themselves.

As these scans produced an absolute replica at a quantum level, it included a complete set of the memories and sense of self, stored within the actual physical matrix of the chemistry of each of their brains, and so the new versions of themselves would be them in pretty much every sense of the word, just different atoms.

The band would never have survived any attempt to match the speed of the passing starship, or cross the temporal distortion surrounding it, never mind the levels of radiation they would be exposed to in interstellar space, or the psychological pressure of being enclosed in an interstellar space craft for years on end. It was far better to copy them in their entirety, transmit it to the ship and allow them to be 're-printed' out of the stardust that the ship had steadily collected across its massive voyage, in time to arrive at Eridani 3. Of course, it was important that the re-printed versions did not realise that they were copies of the originals, as that would undermine their own sense of entitlement to the adoration that they would receive, and as such the illusion of the transit to the HSS2 had to be created, along with elements of their journey on board. Of course, for Danny, this was a pretty normal life experience, he had been copied, one way or another, many many times throughout the millions of years of human life on Earth, and in other forms across other planets throughout space and time, but still he understood that it could all be quite disconcerting when not used to it.

Unfortunately for the actual band, as they remained on Earth, the illusion, up to the point of arriving on the HSS_2 and climbing into the transit suits on board, had to be constructed if they were to embed properly into the copies. Danny realised that they would undoubtedly be hugely disappointed, upset and most likely angry once they realised that they had been tricked and that they would be staying on Earth as it got dragged in around the orbit of the arriving Black Hole. Danny was not looking forward to awakening them from the induced coma inside the scanning suits and being the focus of what would undoubtedly be a difficult moment, and so he wandered about, fiddling about with bits of tools lying on the workshop table, putting a few in pots on shelves and straightening up others. Finally a quiet alarm went off, indicating that the transfer had been completed, and so, with a deep sigh and a shrug, he headed back towards the mock up space shuttle, triggering the door as he approached.

As he waited for the door to open, he continued to shuffle until suddenly another, quite distinct alarm came from the watch on his wrist. Momentarily Danny froze, looked down at his wrist and gently smiled to himself 'well, well, well' he muttered to himself 'well, at least that's something'. He pulled himself up and walked into the shuttle.

'It's ok' said Shadow 'I wasn't completely convinced, I just hope the new version of me will be'

The others were altogether less sanguine, with Georgia the worst – she was well and truly pissed off with Danny and he felt rather disappointed that that would really be the end of that.

'Honestly, you mutant dick fest – I can't believe I fell for that, what an absolute bag of modshite'.

'Steady now, no need for that kind of language' warned Red

Georgia stormed towards what she thought was the exit, only to discover it was a doorway into a storeroom, so went inside anyway and started throwing and kicking things around.

'Anyway' said Danny, 'There is at least one thing that should cheer you all up, if you would all like to follow me, I think you might like this.'

Red called back to Georgia as Danny headed off to the actual exit and started along the short corridor 'We should be just in time for dawn' called Danny over his shoulder as the entire band traipsed dejectedly behind him. He rounded the corner and pulled on another trombone slide sticking out of the wall and the wall started to separate and as it did so a beam of bright yellow light shone along the floor of the corridor and up the far wall. As the door opened more, the bright light filled the space, shining on all the various bits of old musical instruments, and other antique paraphernalia which made up the walls of the workshop.

For the first time ever, the band felt the real warmth of the sun, the light breeze of a spring morning and the smells of the city and countryside beyond.

'The Now Wave passed while you were being copied, you're in the present' said Danny simply 'riding the wave'.

The band wandered out, truly amazed at the intensity of the world that now surrounded them.

'But you said we were one of the least likely continuum's that could ever become a reality – you said we were right out on the edge of what could be' Said Kato, as he looked about truly amazed.

'Yes, well' said Danny 'But the entirety of life on Earth is right out there on the edge of what could be, just imagine, the incredible odds against two single celled creatures merging in just such a way that it was sustainable and mutually beneficial, and then that single cell multiplying enough times before being destroyed that it then completely dominates all other life forms and then creating the huge variety of plant and animal life on Earth. Until eventually it makes human beings, capable of complex thought, collapsing wave functions and then building a civilisation surviving like humanity on Earth for thousands of years – it's like playing, and winning, the lottery every week for an entire lifetime; so one more completely unlikely pathway is not that remarkable. The most interesting thing is that, as it passed you were inside the suits, you were protected from the firestorm of the Now Wave and can therefore remember being virtual before being actual, which is really quite unusual'.

'And what about you' enquired Shadow

'Oh, well the version of me you knew before was completely destroyed, I am the actual version of me that was always riding the Now Wave, but I generally see things from multiple perspectives anyway, so it's pretty much all the same to me'.

He turned and looked over at the club, just the other side of the windswept yard. 'It's quite a place isn't it' he said quietly 'shall we just go and have a last drink before the black hole arrives?'

The band looked at each other and shrugged 'Why not' said Shadow as he picked up his Sax and hitched it back onto his shoulder before gliding effortlessly over to the front door of the club and going inside.

The **My Funny Quarantine** live recording can be heard across all good digital platforms throughout all space and time. More data can be collected at myfunnyquarantine.co.uk

Illustrations by Ruby and Grace Sharp.

Photos from the Band on the Wall archive

Dedicated to everyone who worked so incredibly hard on creating Band on the Wall 3.0 during the pandemic of 2020, along with my family...and Bob and Doug who's inaugural flight to the ISS provided the spark...

Printed in Great Britain
by Amazon